I, Liar

I, Liar

Janice Erlbaum

Thought Catalog Books
Brooklyn, NY

Published by Thought Catalog Books, a division of The Thought & Expression Co.,
Williamsburg, Brooklyn

For general information address hello@thoughtcatalog.com; for submissions to Thought
Catalog Books manuscripts@thoughtcatalog.com

Founded in 2010, Thought Catalog is a website and imprint dedicated to your ideas and
stories

We publish fiction and non-fiction from emerging and established writers across all
genres. Learn more at www.thoughtcatalog.com/about

Cover Art by Daniella Urdinlaiz

Cover Photos by © DinaTulchevska / © ajt

for the girls

It takes two to lie: One to lie, and one to listen.

– Homer

Contents

Also by Janice Erlbaum

PART I

BETH

1994

Borne This Way

I was in second grade when I realized a few things.

1. Sick people are more interesting than well ones.
2. When you are sick, you are excused from doing everything you're supposed to do.
3. The nurse's office is an excellent place to spend an hour, lying peacefully on a cot in a darkened room until someone turns on the light and puts their hand on your forehead and asks, "Do you feel a little bit better now, Sweetie?" And if not, they call your mother at the salon, and let you lie there until she can come get you and take you home.
4. You can make yourself pass out by inhaling magic markers.

The first time I passed out, it was an accident. I was sitting in the art room of my suburban grade school with my fellow seven-year-olds, making posters on the topic of school safety using those magic markers that were scented according to their color. I loved those markers, the synesthesia they inspired – it made so much sense that colors had smells, that black smelled like licorice and yellow like a lemon. I loved the way the green scent of mint passed through my nose and landed on the back of my tongue.

And, as with everything else I loved, I had to overdo it, so I wasn't drawing anything on my poster, concentrating instead on jamming the markers as far up my nose as they could go without pain so I could smell them *the most*.

As I sniffed deeply, I started to feel...separate, somehow. The way I felt when I repeated a word too many times and it turned into gibberish, sound without meaning. Like, why would we call a thing a "garage?" Garage, garage, garage, garage...

The red marker was so far up my nostril, I was on the verge of a sneeze. I felt something important starting to rise to the surface in my mind but I was distracted by its importance, and the cherry smell of red, and I was swooning, leaning into it, this crucial thought I very much wanted to have, and just as it was about to come to me...

I was lying on my back on the art room floor with everyone clustered around me freaking out.

How I wish I could have seen it from the other kids' point of view. How exciting it would have been, to watch one of my classmates swoon and slip beneath the lip of the crafts table, to hear their sudden, heavy body hit the floor, to see their blank eyes and think they might be dead. To scream, to watch the teacher scramble to the felled child–the slapping of the face, the yelling of the name, and then...my eyes flutter open. Alive!

Two decades later, I am right there: Everyone's shocked-wide eyes, the supersonic crackle of expended fear, the susurration of relief. The pain in the back of my head from where it hit the floor – its astonishing, ultraviolet clarity, the purple taste of pain. The pain I earned.

After that, I found a way to make myself pass out in every new school I attended up until fifth grade, and I attended plenty. Smelling markers, hyperventilating, standing up while holding my breath–it went over huge every time. But I always knew, as I was preparing to faint, that I was about to miss the most exciting part of the movie. Such is the price of being the star.

———

Please understand: I wasn't born bad.

I was born lonely. I had no father, and half a mother, at best – had we not lived with her parents during my first three years, I doubt I would have survived her neglect. In her defense, she was young, and single, and "she did the best she could." Which is a meaningless tautology, especially to a five-year-old who's left alone in her room for hours with her blankie and the TV while her mother entertains her married boss.

I don't blame my mother for everything, just her awful genes and her horrible parenting. The rest of the responsibility is mine. There's something essential that's driven me for as long as I can remember; one day, it'll drive me into my grave. I have always needed too much love.

"You were a difficult baby," my mother liked to say. "You cried all the time. You were never satisfied."

This is her version of the story: I was a difficult baby. Deficient. I'm not sure whether that makes me the chicken or the egg in the which-came-first of our relationship, whereby my excessive need for love caused my mother to love me less, causing my excessive need for love, causing her to love me less, but my mother always implied it originated with me, the egg. Even though she's the one who hatched me.

I had few friends in my early youth. After leaving her parents' house, my mother moved us from man to man and place to place, and every time, she said the same thing: "This is good, it's a new start. You didn't like that last school anyway."

She always did this – she acted like it wasn't her best interest but my best interest she had in mind, which was laughable, not that I dared laugh. We weren't moving again because I didn't like my school – I'd liked both of my kindergartens well enough, and both of my first grades, and the first of my second grades, and we'd still moved away.

However, my second second grade was not going very well at all. It started promisingly enough – I was the new kid again, but this time my mother got the idea to put me on the school bus on my third day with cupcakes to pass out to everyone at lunch, "for my birthday" (which was actually three weeks prior, in August). Thus I was not stuck standing alone at recess for long.

But within weeks, I'd painted myself into a corner with my

promises and lies. If I did in fact have a pony at my house, my peers demanded, it was time for me to produce it. If I was in fact a ballet dancer, it was time for me to prove that I could dance ballet.

I'd become so used to moving around that I'd never had to back up my stories before – by the time any proof was required of me, I'd already moved on to the next place. Now I was stuck here, knee-deep in my own poop, no longer welcome to discuss television shows or trade stickers with my classmates, and the only game I got to play at recess was Keep Away. My teacher wouldn't even let me go to the nurse anymore.

So yes, maybe it was a good thing this time that my mother was tired of...whichever one it was. Rudy? Dean? Stu? Whoever. They were all just a bunch of shins to me: hairy shins in shorts in the summer, clad shins at the door in the evening, naked shins coming out of the shower. Shins that passed in the night.

I don't remember which boyfriend she was leaving, or which New Jersey suburb we were in, but I definitely remember riding shotgun in her old burgundy Toyota as she told me we'd be moving again, and I'm pretty sure I felt relief at the idea, though I would not admit it.

"I don't want to go to another school," I complained.

"Excuse me?" My mother stole a look at herself in the rear view mirror while we idled at a red light, flashing that subconscious mirror-face she always made: slight pout, chin tucked, eyes wide. She looked at me via the mirror. "You have to go to school, it's the law."

I sank lower in my seat, sulking. I shifted my attention to the button that controlled the window, placing my finger in its sensuous depression. Things like this calmed me down, the idea that some unseen person had anticipated my finger and made the button smooth for me, and I was closing a circuit by fulfilling their prediction.

"Why can't we go back and live with Grandma and Grandpa?"

My mother emitted a puff of air in lieu of a laugh. "I'm not going back to that," she said, as though our lives in Florida had been terrible, as though we didn't have a pool and three cars and a little red tricycle for me.

"Why?" I whined.

She pressed her lips into a hard line. "I wouldn't have been stuck living there in the first place if it hadn't been for you," she said. As though she'd done me a favor, one I'd owe her for the rest of my life.

My mother—or, what the hell, let's call her Annabel; I'm a grown woman now, at least her equal – is what people call "sharp," as in shrewd, canny, and mercenary in the service of her needs. She is not book-smart, nor does she care to be (the sign of true unintelligence), but she is people-smart. My mother can talk her way out of anything, manipulate anyone into doing her bidding. She can charm snakes, because she is one.

I inherited many things from her: her nose for opportunity, her keen desire to "get hers." Like her, I am angry all the time, and like her, I am doubly angry at being forced to feel anger, so it compounds. The phrase "grim determination" comes to mind, both of us stomping up escalators, cursing furiously while trying to parallel park, charging across the street against the light because we refuse to stand there for forty-five seconds being thwarted.

One thing I didn't inherit is her looks, which is probably a good thing. Pretty people often attract the wrong kind of attention. I'm not looking for sex, and I don't want it looking for me. And what if I'd been able to skate by on the barest effort, like her, exploiting the fabulous luck of my looks, and people paid attention to me all the time even though I wasn't interesting or insightful or worthwhile in any way? Well, that would have been tragic.

My father, whoever he was, must have been very brilliant and very ugly, in order to counteract my sometimes quite stupid mother's stunning good looks.

———

My mother's boyfriends took up a disproportionate amount of her time, and I envied them for it. I wished *I* could be my mother's boyfriend – a wish that placed me in a hazy grey zone somewhere between Oedipus and Electra, where I have loitered ever since – but that was impractical.

When I was finishing out the school year in my third second grade, my mother met and quickly married a man named Chuck, as in, "to throw." I was encouraged to call him "Uncle Chuck," but both of those words nauseated me, so most often I addressed him as "Ummm..." Chuck had little use for me – to him, I was like a chihuahua my mother happened to own – and I had no use for him, but I will admit that living with him was nicer than any other place we'd lived, even Grandma and Grandpa's.

The new three-bedroom house in Short Hills, New Jersey had a marble shower with six nozzles that stuck out from every height and direction. My room had a "Juliet balcony," and Chuck bought me a new white canopy bed with gold trim and a dresser and desk to match. Downstairs, there was a den for watching TV, and next to that was Chuck's office, where he spent hours on the phone braying about his shady real estate deals.

After several failed attempts at gainful matrimony, my mother had struck gold with Chuck. He was older, rich, generous, and insecure; always antsy, jingling the coins in his pocket – "A go-getter," Annabel said, and he certainly go-got her most everything she asked for: a car, a credit card, a purebred Persian kitten who had to be returned because it vomited hairballs on the rug. She was his knockout new wife, and he wanted to take her everywhere, which meant she took on fewer hours at the salon, which soon meant no hours at all, which was just fine with her.

Chuck the Shmuck. He called me "Kiddo." Like I was a dog, or a Marx brother. He was that kind of guy. "Hey, Kiddo, why don't you grab me the remote." The kind of guy who wore Hawaiian shirts that pooched over his beltless belly, and hummed along too loudly to music in stores. The kind of guy who, if you asked him how he was doing, might actually spend three minutes telling you some story about the guy who was supposed to clean the gutters, and how the guy didn't show up, and how you can't trust "these people," "these people" meaning non-white laborers, then expect you to share his outrage.

Once in the very beginning I tested him a little, gave him some sassy attitude at the Chinese restaurant where we were having our get-to-know-you supper. Because, come on – he wasn't even trying to include me in the conversation. All I got from him was, "So you're Annabel's kid," and, "Your mother says you like to read a lot of books, huh?" and then it was like I wasn't even there.

Fifteen minutes of being ignored and shut out. Nobody even looked my way. I could have stuck a chopstick in my eye, they wouldn't have cared. I was fuming, so hot I was sticking to the plastic banquette. How could they not notice this? How could they not see me? I started swinging my legs under the table. When that failed to attract their attention, I began to hum. My mother, still hanging on Chuck's every word, reached out under the table and gave my leg a pinch.

I stopped humming and sulked for a second. She didn't care. I squeezed my eyes tight to make myself cry. She didn't notice. Chuck kept telling some boring business story that had already gone on way too long and showed no sign of ever ending.

I said loudly, "Your name should be Upchuck."

This was the kind of thing kids said on sitcoms, and everybody laughed, because it's hilarious to hear young children mouth off to some jackass and say the thing everybody else wished they could say.

Chuck drew back a little and looked confusedly at my mother. Had my joke gone over his head? It was like he didn't understand the words I said, or he didn't hear them, or he was stumped by the presence of this child at his table, or he was baffled by the very idea of children. What a dumb face he was making: squinting, his mouth slightly agape.

My mother asked him to excuse us a moment, grabbed me by the upper arm, and took me to the ladies' room, where she swung me around to face her.

"What the hell are you doing," she hissed.

"Nothing."

"I swear to God, you want to go live with your Grandma? Keep this up and you'll get your wish. I'll put you on the plane tomorrow, if you don't cut it out."

Her grip was too tight on my arm. Why did I always get everything so wrong? This wasn't what I wanted at all. I didn't want to live with Grandma unless my mom was going to be there too. I didn't want to make her mad, I didn't want her to want me to go away. The only reason I'd piped up at all was because they were ignoring me. I started to cry.

"Beth," she said. "*Do not do this now.* You will not get what you want."

When she put it like that, one pragmatist to another, I could not deny its truth. This was not a winning tactic. She simply wasn't going to put up with any impediment to her relationship with Chuck. She wanted Chuck more than she wanted me, and if Chuck didn't want me, she'd get rid of me.

This alarming idea made me cry even harder, but I was already nodding and trying to stop. "I'm sorry," I said. "I'm sorry. I'll be better. I'm sorry."

I had to find a role for myself in the new arrangement. I had to be useful enough to compensate for the inconvenience I caused by existing. Fortunately, I noted that my mother lacked someone to gloat with about her good fortune. Her friend Fern from the salon was suitably envious when she came for brunch that time, mouthing *oh my God*, and *I hate you*, but Fern wasn't around every day like I was. Grandma didn't have much to say during her monthly phone calls besides, "The house sounds very lovely," which for some reason enraged my mother – "*It is!*"

So I was the only one Annabel could half-turn to, narrating from the driver's seat of the new black BMW; I was the mirror with the flattering light.

"Can you believe this?" she marveled to me, speeding home from the mall with a backseat full of bags. "Six months ago we were in that godforsaken shack with Stu."

I thought about Stu's "cottage" in Atlantic City: the rusted screens, the mildewed furniture. The bathroom we all shared and nobody cleaned. "This is *a lot* better," I said.

She smiled, satisfied, and regarded me side-eyed. "You know it."

When she did deign to smile upon me – or, rather, upon herself in the rear view mirror over something I said – I hated how much I liked it.

"I love my bedroom," I said. "I love the swing set."

From the way her chin rose, I knew this pleased her.

This was my first taste of the crack cocaine that is maternal attention. This feeling of being wanted, liked, useful, necessary, and most of all, *secure*. Too often my mother regarded me as though I were a changeling, not the daughter she'd ordered, but my gushing over furniture proved that I wasn't hopeless, that I recognized what had value in the world, that I was her daughter after all. For the first time in my short life, I started to feel like I might have some job security as my mother's daughter. Maybe I could stop waiting for her to fire me out of the blue.

2

The Wrong Road

Chuck's house – *our* house – was a five-minute ride on the yellow bus from my new school, where I attended my first third grade. I began the grade with the rest of my class right after Labor Day – another fresh start, which meant "birthday" cupcakes for the whole class within that first week, at which my new teacher frowned and said, "Your record says your birthday was in August."

I froze, skin tingling. "What?"

"Your birthday was in August," she repeated. "Not today."

I was flabbergasted. I had never been challenged like this before, by an adult I'd just met and had barely even lied to yet. The unfairness of it – that she would accuse me of something that, as far as she knew, I didn't even do! Something that wasn't even my idea! It was my mom's idea! Tears came to my eyes, and I almost threw myself on the floor and started bawling, but I knew I couldn't crack like that.

"No," I insisted, loud and indignant. "It's my birthday today."

My teacher looked into my eyes and raised her eyebrows. "Really."

"Yeah."

She stared at me, assessing me, which was galling, but I wouldn't look away. She raised her chin, so I raised mine. Her eyes narrowed, and I could hear her thinking, *This kid is lying while looking me right in the eye. Damn.* Like she was impressed despite herself. She nodded at me the way one gunfighter nods to another in Westerns: I see you, and I will deal with you later.

"Okay," she said.

While she couldn't stop the kids from taking my cupcakes, she had managed to taint them with suspicion: My cupcakes were a fraud, and so was I. Soon, I would be duly ostracized by the members of my class, and in record time – I lost the battle for credibility in the first three days.

Fortunately, there was Lillian.

Lillian Miller was a fiercely motivated eight-year-old with an excellent vocabulary who could read as well and quickly as I could, which had never happened in any school before. At first I hated her guts for it, so much so that my body squirmed and twisted without my consent, and sometimes when she was reading something aloud, I'd find myself on the literal edge of my seat, rocking my crotch against the curved rim of my wooden chair, driven by a furious urge.

One of the earliest dreams I remember having was about Lillian. She was cruelly taunting me, and I became enraged, so I lunged at her and bit off a huge chunk of her skull, like the size of an apple. Then I spit it out, and then suddenly there were all these other people around, yelling at me. And I realized with despair, *Holy shit, I'm in trouble for the rest of my life.*

That phase of despising her was so vivid, it consumed me physically, left me breathless. It felt like I was running a race for the right to exist. Nobody needed *two* smart, weird, unhappy eight-year-old girls who read way above grade level; one of us was redundant. I had to be better than her or I would die.

One day at recess, we were both on the outskirts of the playground, dawdling by the same tree. She squatted and picked up a stick and started scratching the earth around the tree's roots.

"I'm digging a secret underground clubhouse," she announced.

Immediately, I picked up a stick of my own and began digging next to her. I was now the vice-president of this club, and any other club she cared to create.

Lillian had dark hair and thick lashes and skin that looked tan, even in winter, with the softest hairs in a line down her backbone that you could only see in the sunlight. Jesus, she was a miscreant. And so magnificent. Just her name – Lillian – she sounded like a *grand dame*, or a soap opera villain. I had never been so enamored of any person as I was of her, not even my mother. I'd never felt such synchrony as I did when in her presence.

Lillian was the first person I'd ever recognized as being like me. What that meant, I didn't yet know.

———

"Let's walk home," Lillian said one afternoon early into our friendship, as we readied to go to the school bus. *Her* home, she meant, a few streets away from mine, but I'd played at her house after school two or three times so far, and it was already home to me.

"Okay."

The walk was long for our short legs, but it was fun, because we weren't supposed to do it. Anything we could put past adults was a victory. Lillian understood this implicitly in a way other kids did not. She knew it was us against them. She believed in hoarding the loose change her parents left around, stealing a pack of gum while buying a candy bar, sneaking one of the class erasers into the garbage and looking wide-eyed around the room with the other kids – where could the eraser have gone?

I adored her. She was chaos in a pair of Keds. She was a genius, and she made me feel like a genius, too. I have barely any recollection of anything from those few months but Lillian. It's probably best that way.

We made poison in her backyard: a puddle of mud, a squished caterpillar, and some torn-up ivy leaves from her mother's trellis, stirred with a stick.

"Ivy is *really, really* poison," she said seriously, scooping up the puddle with a clear plastic cup. "That's why it's 'poison ivy.'"

"Yeah," I agreed. "We could give it to our teacher."

"We should give it to Pippa."

Pippa was the six-year-old baby tattletale next door who was always hanging around us, then crying to her mother when we sent her away: "They're being mean to me, tell them they have to be nice to me!" Pippa interrupted at inopportune times, like when we were playing the naked game. Pippa was an impediment to our happiness and self-expression, so our desire to poison her to death was entirely her own fault.

"We *should* give it to Pippa."

Women of action, we rose at once and set out with our plastic cup of poison, but for once, Pippa was nowhere to be found, so we could not kill her, and she lived to annoy us another day.

Who we *should* have poisoned was Lillian's loathsome, creepy brother, Mark, age twelve, who was nominally "in charge" of us in the afternoons until her parents got home from work, or whatever it was that adults did all day, not that it mattered. To me, adults were either present or not present, and all I cared about was being where they were not.

The adults were not present at Lillian's. Mark was often busy playing video games by himself (or, less often, with friends); on those days, Lillian and I were left to our own devices. Then came the day he burst in on us when we were playing the naked game in her bedroom without the door locked, and since then he'd been tormenting us, threatening to reveal our shame and ignominy to "everybody" if we didn't do what he said.

No matter how many ice cream sandwiches were fetched from the freezer, no matter what degrading phrases he forced us to say in order to buy his silence, he still sang at Lillian, "I'm telling Mom you were *na*ked." To me, it was, "I saw your *pu*ssy." He learned the word from a magazine he kept hidden in his room, which we tried to steal at every opportunity, both for the leverage it would have given us over him and for research.

Mark was the evil version of Lillian: just as intense and driven, but with malicious intent. He had a small folding knife he liked to fold and unfold in front of us. What a psychopath. I know for a fact that he threw rocks at squirrels, and who does that besides a psychopath? Say what you will about me, but I have never harmed an animal. Nor would I sexually menace a child – two children, even, one his own sister.

Meanwhile, school. Lillian's desk had been placed on the opposite side of the room from mine, blocking our sight lines. Still, we managed to pop up and peer around like prairie dogs to grimace at each other in the middle of class. The teacher loathed us, but our grades were excellent, even with the demerits for "fooling around" and "not paying attention," so there wasn't much she could do.

And all the between-times – lunch and recess and gym and assembly and the five minutes before the bell rang in the morning and we had to be in our seats, everyone, in our SEATS, PLEASE, Lillian, Beth...LILLIAN, BETH – those times were all ours.

One November afternoon at recess, we were hanging around by the tree that would one day shelter our underground clubhouse, once the weather got better and we renewed our commitment to digging.

"We should run away," Lillian said.

"YES," I agreed.

She always had the best ideas. One day as we were walking home from school, she suggested we ring somebody's doorbell and ask if we could use the bathroom, which went brilliantly--a kindly grey-haired lady invited us into her home and let us use the upstairs toilet. A pointless victory, on the surface. It's not like we stole anything or she gave us home-baked cookies or whatever. I didn't even have to pee. It was just another caper to commit.

I'd thought of running away before. Once, when I was five and we were living in Metuchen, New Jersey, I decided, *fuck all this shit*, and I walked out the garage door and hid under an overturned garbage can for a while, my shoe wedged under the rim for a sliver of light and air. Then I got hot and claustrophobic and went back in the house.

Now I was more prepared. I hadn't even known how prepared I was until Lillian suggested it, and right away I realized, *I've been planning for this*. Now, with my best friend by my side, it was a *fait accompli*. We were running away the first opportunity we got.

"My mom will be so mad," said Lillian. "She'll say it's my brother's fault for not watching us better, and he'll be in so much trouble."

"They'll all be sad, too, because we went away."

We jumped up and down and clutched each other with excitement. How wonderful it would be: My mother crying because she'd lost me, realizing she loved me, swearing to make everything up to me if only I'd return. How delicious an idea, one I could suck on the way I sucked on the fatness of my tongue, gluing it to my palate. ("Don't do that," my mother told me. "It makes your face look weird.")

We decided to bring money, food, a flashlight, some underwear, and the transitional object of our choice, mine being a bear that I can't even stand to think about because, twenty years later, I will collapse with grief over its loss. We would take as much money from our parents as we could – not just the change left strewn on the dresser, but the change in the change jar, the change from their pockets, and if any paper money was pilferable, that too – and we'd get the food from our cabinets and fridges.

"We could go to New York," I said. The obvious choice for people running away from New Jersey. The city was only forty minutes by car, we'd both been driven there enough times to know how to get to the parkway, and from there, we'd just follow the signs. When we got to the city, we'd tell people we were orphans – "sisters" – looking for a new family. We'd both read the book about the girl who runs away and lives in the Metropolitan Museum of Art, and it worked out just fine for her.

Once we'd given voice to the idea, we could not wait to execute it. We decided we'd acquire ten dollars a piece as fast as possible without getting caught, and when we hit our goal, we'd wake up the next morning, raid our fridges, and (in lieu of our books) put the food in our schoolbags with the other supplies. Then we'd meet on the corner by school, and start walking the other direction. By the time anyone noticed we were absent and attempted to confirm this with our parents, we'd be halfway to the George Washington Bridge: me, and my partner in crime.

———

I must have known something was coming at home. I didn't know it consciously, and nothing explicit was said to me, but I must have understood that Chuck was getting tired of me, which meant Annabel would soon need me gone. On the surface, she could still be affectionate towards me, mostly so whatever repulsion she felt towards me didn't show. That wouldn't reflect well on either of us. What kind of monster doesn't love her own daughter? And what kind of unlovable monster child had she produced?

My mother's affection was almost worse than her disregard. At least the disregard felt genuine. In her eagerness to spin me as not-entirely-undesirable, she had taken to primping me – fluffing my hair, fixing my clothes, using a spit-covered finger to wipe a smudge off my face – while touting to Chuck my "creativity" and my "intelligence." Thus she translated a note from my teacher saying that I was being disruptive in class into me being "too smart for my grade level," and "not challenged enough."

"They said she's got the math and reading skills to skip at least one grade, if not two," she told Chuck, picking some shmutz off my shirt and smoothing it, making the merchandise look its best. I perked up at this news – though I would never leave my class as long as Lillian was in it, I liked confirmation that I was so far above average, and the idea of being in a class full of older students was attractive. I pictured being the smallest, the most deserving of the teacher's attention, the most special.

As it turned out, nobody had suggested that I skip a grade, as I discovered when I told my mother I wanted to do so.

"You're not skipping anything," she said. "Now brush your hair, you look like a crazy person."

Is it hackneyed if I say that I wanted my mother to love me? I've spent years in therapists' offices talking about her (her narcissism, her cruelty, her refusal to talk about my father) and the nearly fatal effect she had on me, but I am starting to think it might be as simple as this: I wanted her to love me. Because – and this is the really hard part to admit, after I've spent decades telling myself and everybody else the opposite – I loved her.

Some of that was purely biology: my physical desire to be held by her, the way I wanted to nestle into her smell. But some of that was Annabel. She had charisma. Everybody who met her got it. She was brave, and unafraid to break rules, because she was superior to the dumb, slow, ordinary people the rules were made for. She could be hilarious, especially when she was being mean about somebody else. Times like that, I wanted to be her best friend.

And she was *so* good at her trade. I sat on the sidelines marveling at her finesse as she played her honey-vinegar games with Chuck the drone. For instance: When she didn't get something she wanted from Chuck – though I'm having trouble trying to remember an instance of that happening – well, let's say he didn't want to take her someplace she wanted to go. A lesser woman might try pouting, or baby talk, or sex, or the silent treatment. Not Annabel.

No, whatever the bone of contention was, my mother immediately let it go, and if you had not grown up with her every day of your life since birth, studying her face for clues to the moods that would affect your fate, you would not see even the slightest shadow pass her brow. A tiny bit of the left corner of her mouth might hitch a little higher, her smile teetering on the boundary of smirk territory, but if you didn't know her as well as I do, you'd never catch it.

The next morning, she'd make a big show of being loving and doting. She'd say, apropos of nothing, how very lucky she was and how very happy she felt and how very grateful she was to Chuck for making this all come to pass. You'd think she had no recollection of any discord the night before, or if she did recollect it, she'd realized she was just being silly and selfish and was doing her best to make up for it. He would leave for his day with endearments tickling his ear, feeling kingly.

Now *this* is people smart. You always want to make people feel good before you make them feel bad. My mother, as I've mentioned, can't multiply numbers without a calculator, but it doesn't matter, because she knows how to push buttons. The carrot and the stick is not an either-or game, the way some people play it. No – first you give them a big whiff of the carrot, then you beat them with it like a stick.

To wit: He'd come home that night, and she'd be ever so slightly sad. She'd still smile at him, bravely, and make her usual fuss, but he'd be able to tell there was something wrong. It's nothing, she'd tell him, when he finally mentioned it. (Sigh.) Just her being dumb, as usual. Just feeling a little...oh, it's nothing.

Another crucial point here: You have to make him coax it out of you. You have to make him feel like you don't want to bother him with your petty feelings. This is *not* the silent treatment; you keep talking, you just change the subject. But a man like Chuck will "see right through" your attempts to deceive him, because he is a savvy businessman who can read people, that's what he does for a living, so if something is the matter with his beautiful girl, he's going to ferret it out of her.

I would watch this slo-mo chase unfold over the course of an evening. She'd ask him how that thing was going, that important business thing he'd been dealing with. She'd get him to tell her a story in which he triumphed over someone who was trying to bamboozle him. She'd pour a few fingers of brown booze from the decanter, but her hands would be slightly shaky, and she'd gulp hard to suppress something that was plaguing her...

"Bel," he'd say. "Tell me what's the matter."

And she'd dip her head and smile ruefully. Of course a guy as savvy as Chuck wasn't going to be fooled by her act. She shouldn't have tried to hide things from him. It's just that she knew she was being stupid, she knew it was nothing, she didn't want to rock the boat in any way, because (extra points if she could effect a tremble in her voice, a tear in her eye, as she searched for the right way to say it)...

"I'm so afraid of losing you. I already feel like I don't deserve you. No, it's true. I don't. I try to, I really do, I just..."

Soothe, soothe. Coax, coax.

"It's just, you've been so wonderful and generous and I don't know why I get insecure sometimes, I just love you so much, and I can't understand why you'd want to be with me. You're a real estate tycoon – no, it's true! And I'm a single mom who cuts hair."

"Bel, baby," he'd remind her. "You're not single anymore."

Oh, she'd done it again! She said something stupid! Of course she wasn't single anymore, and see, that's why she was so afraid she would do or say the wrong thing – not because she meant to, just because she was dumb and uneducated and not as good as him in any way. And while he was always so sweet to her and never gave her any indication that he felt anything but overwhelming adoration for her, every once in a while she'd get paranoid for no reason that he was losing interest in her, like for instance if he didn't want to take her out to that thing she wanted to go to last night. And she knew it was stupid, she knew *she* was stupid, and sometimes she thought she should just get out of his life and leave him free to find someone more worthy than her...

Here is the subtext, in case you're a moron like Chuck: I'm thinking of leaving you because you don't love me enough, as you proved by not taking me to the thing last night.

And he'd fall for it! He would rush to impress upon her just how much he did love her, how fantastic she was, to apologize for making her ever doubt him. And here she'd refuse to hear his apology – "No, don't apologize, you didn't do anything wrong, it was all me!" – denying him the forgiveness he asked for and leaving a dangling thread of guilt in his mind.

I appreciate this now in a way I couldn't then: the elegance of it, the nuance. I myself was sometimes fooled into sympathizing with this adorable insecure woman who thought she wasn't good enough to be loved. The long-term thinking she had to engage in, the patience it must have taken. I wish I'd known enough to say to her: *I see what you did there, Mom, and that was a master stroke.*

Maybe if she'd known how much I could appreciate her, she would have appreciated me. Or maybe if I'd been a different type of girl, someone more like her in looks and temperament. If I was pretty, I bet she would have taken me through every page of her playbook, pointing out the different ways to combine x's and o's in order to score; she might have even recognized my own talent for gamesmanship. We could have been a team.

———

It took two days for me and Lillian to get the money we needed, then it was time for us to hit the road. We met on the assigned corner that morning, grinning like maniacs, and started walking away talking to each other with our heads bent together like always, except in the wrong direction. If any adult asked where we were going, we could pretend we'd been so deep in conference we hadn't noticed we were headed the wrong way.

Were we afraid of getting caught? I was. I was dizzy with it. I wasn't wholly sure this was all happening, that we were now a full three blocks from school and were going to keep going. I expected an adult to stop us at any moment. I wasn't going to admit to being scared; the few times I'd done so in our relationship, Lillian had become annoyed and demanded, "Don't be scared."

It was an exhilarating fear, at least, and as we walked through the local streets towards the Garden State Parkway, it only got headier. This *was* happening, and nothing could make it un-happen. Even if we wanted to turn back now, we'd be in a world of shit for skipping school, more trouble than either of us had ever seen; with every step, we burned the bridge we walked on, and the road ahead shimmered with its heat.

We discussed the story we'd give the people at the orphanage, or wherever it was we were going. (We'd figure that part out when we got to New York.)

"I want my name to be Lisa," I said. I was obsessed with the name Lisa. I thought it was the number one prettiest name for a girl.

"I'm keeping my name," said Lillian. "But my last name is...Sammy. Lillian Sammy."

"I'm Lisa Sammy," I said. "Cause we're sisters."

We linked the pinkies we'd stabbed on multiple occasions to mix our blood in her bedroom. "For real now."

It took about forty-five minutes for us to navigate the local streets. And to this day, I wonder how many cars passed right by us, two unaccompanied eight-year-olds walking along busy thoroughfares without sidewalks in the middle of a weekday. Did nobody think, *Well, this is odd*? I remain amazed that nobody stopped and offered us a ride, neither a concerned citizen nor a child molester.

When we finally reached the on-ramp to the parkway, we stopped short: A sign we'd never noticed said NO PEDESTRIANS. We hadn't known we'd be breaking the law by walking the parkway.

"We'll say we don't know what 'pedestrian' means," Lillian

decided, and I agreed. Most kids our age didn't know what a pedestrian was; that's how pedestrian they were.

So we forged ahead down the ramp and started walking along the grassy embankment on the New York-bound side of the road.

The sun was getting higher in the sky. We hadn't brought any water with us, and just thinking about the saltines with peanut butter I had in my bag made me feel parched. I was realizing that I would have to pee at some point, probably soon. But then I looked to my left, and there was Lillian, trudging along right next to me, making little noises of effort and smelling like little-kid sweat, and I felt buoyed with happiness and hope.

I wonder what would have happened to me if I'd never met Lillian. I wonder if I could have settled for normal relationships with normal people, if I'd never had the love of my life to compare them to. She's the only person I ever met who didn't find me "too intense," who knew exactly what I was thinking because she was thinking the same thing. There had always been a burning in me, but Lillian turned up the flame.

When the black and white police car pulled over to the shoulder of the parkway in front of us, I burst into tears. A policeman got out of the passenger side door and stood there with his hands on his hips. "Hello, ladies," he said, unsmiling. "Where are we going today?"

———

This would be the last time we were ever together, me and Lillian Miller, riding in the backseat of a police car to the station, where we were separated, interviewed, and returned to our respective homes. We didn't say anything to each other in the car – I doubt I could have spoken over my sobbing. She wasn't crying; if anything, she looked pissed that we'd been caught, and proud. I wonder if she likes to tell people now, as I do, the story about being busted as an eight-year-old runaway on the Garden State Parkway.

I'd ask her, if I could find her to ask. I've looked her up many times – she was the first person I looked for when I got online

– but I've never found her. Back then, that wasn't too strange, but in 2014, to be unfindable is suspicious. It means you don't want to be found, and who doesn't want to be found? My alibi is airtight: I'm not on social media because of "what happened in high school." I wonder what her story is.

Maybe she reformed, and doesn't want any trace of her old self to come and haunt her. Maybe that's why she's never tried to find me, as far as I know. She could have simply married someone and changed her name, and that's why I haven't found her. But I'll always remember walking next to Lillian Miller towards the Garden State Parkway, her sharp chin high as she declared, "I'm keeping my name."

3

Foundling in Exile

Five days after I was returned to my mother's home by a uniformed officer of the law, I was sent off at the airport to my Grandma's in Florida.

Annabel was suspiciously prepared for me to do something that would lead to my ouster. The door had hardly closed behind the officer, his parting words about a follow-up visit from Child Protective Services still hanging in the air, when she said, "That settles it." As though a coin had been launched into the air a while ago, and she'd just slapped it down on the back of her hand.

She wasn't even a little bit sorry about it. "You want to run away? You don't want to live here anymore? You got your wish." There was no concern for me, no fervent, "Thank *God* nothing terrible happened to you." Just her snarling and me sobbing, as I had been since the moment Lillian and I were apprehended.

It went on for five minutes or so in that vein: "You brought this on yourself," and "I hope you're happy." Relentless, and the angrier she got the more I cried, and the more I cried the angrier she got. "You're not crying your way out of this one, Elizabeth, so cut it out." Finally she ordered me to, "GET UPSTAIRS RIGHT NOW, AND I DON'T WANT TO SEE YOU FOR THE REST OF THE NIGHT, DO YOU HEAR ME?"

I hate her. I know I said I loved her before, but right now I hate her. Thinking about this poor unhappy child, so unseen at home that she'd put her life in danger trying to run away; this child who'd walked five miles in the sun that day with her teddy bear in her backpack, looking for a glimmer of something resembling love; and now this child is destroyed. *Destroyed.* Words like "hopeless" and "despairing" are inadequate to describe the full-body kinetic sensation of falling through a black hole that widens as it deepens, funneling you into its vortex as it sucks up the entire universe.

I'm sorry. Where was I?

Ah, yes. I was forsaken and devastated on the floor of a bedroom that was once considered mine, and would soon be considered another closet. Then I was waiting outside the school records office while my mother withdrew me. Then I was at the same Chinese restaurant we always went to, having a goodbye dinner with her and Chuck.

Watching Annabel put her arm around me and pet my hair, you might have thought she was sad to see me go, or that she would miss me. Or, once again, that this was in my best interest (it was, but that was coincidence), and not hers. "This will be good for you, Lizzybit. It'll be a good environment."

Perhaps knowing she'd be rid of me soon made her feel more affectionate, my anticipated absence making her heart grow fonder. More likely, she was playing it up for Chuck, making it seem like sending me away was something she was doing for the sake of the relationship. Then whenever she wanted leverage with him, she could sigh and look faraway and wonder how her little girl was doing.

I mean, how else was I going to turn out, with a mother like her? Not only because of how she treated me; because of what she taught me. I couldn't turn my back on the family business, the traditions and skills that she passed down to me. It'd be like a violin prodigy refusing to play.

———

The next day, Annabel drove me to the airport with my two suitcases. It was strange, just the two of us in the car; I hadn't been alone with her in a long time, or so it suddenly seemed.

She had been so hardhearted with me that week – I spent most of the five days between my apprehension and my exile in my room crying, unacknowledged and uncomforted, with no communication beyond curt directions: "Come get dinner." "Time for bed." "Stop it."

Now we had no idea what to say to each other. I had no way to play up to her or make myself useful, which was my usual tack, and she had run out of her customary proclamations about the way the world really works. Sometimes she'd be silent when she was angry at me, but that was the kind of SILENCE that shouts its meaning. This silence lacked conviction. She didn't want to meet my eyes, even to glare.

She *was* angry, of course. Nobody had ever rejected Annabel the way I did. There'd never been a man or a woman who'd decided they had enough of her company before she decided that about them; then again, none of them knew her the way I did. I'd proved that it was justified, even necessary, for her to lie and falsify the way she did – look what happened when someone got a glimpse of the real 'Bel. They ran.

But this wasn't just anger. The way she chewed her bottom lip and cleared her throat and tapped her fingers against the steering wheel – this was fear. And it was because of me. If I hadn't despaired before, I was doing so now – what kind of horror was I, that my own mother was afraid of me? Anger fades with time, but if she was truly afraid of me, she'd never love me.

Once at the airport, my mother shepherded me through security and to the gate, where the female flight attendant behind the desk made a big fuss over me. "Flying alone! You are so grown-up! Well, don't worry, hon, we're all going to take good care of you. Isn't she a doll?" This last bit she addressed to my mother, who smiled and acted as though she liked me even one-tenth as much as this stranger did.

Everything was much easier for Annabel when she was playing a role. With the flight attendant as an audience, she could slip right into the part of Caring Mother, crouching down to my height and looking at me eye-to-eye. It was the first time in a week she'd looked anywhere near my face, except to squint at me with disgust. She had – she *has* – beautiful hazel eyes ringed just at the edge with green, and golden-brown lashes she curls with a special tool. As much as I sometimes wished I was pretty like her, I wished right then that she was ugly like me. It would have been easier not to love her.

"Bethie, I told Grandma to call me as soon as you get off the plane, so I know you made it there okay. So don't let her leave the airport until she's called me! She's going to be so excited to have you, she's going to want to go straight home so she can show you off to her neighbors, and she's going to forget all about me." She made her flirty pouty face – poor Annabel, forgotten again.

"I won't forget," I said, the Doting Daughter.

She laughed and embraced me. "I know you won't forget, because you're my smarty, aren't you, smarty-pants." She stood to her full height and turned her smile to the flight attendant. "I tell you, she could probably fly the plane, this one."

"If you want, Hon, you can see the cockpit," said the attendant. The word made me think of Lillian's brother's magazine.

"No thank you," I said quietly.

My mother made motions to leave, to turn her back and walk away and leave me here with a bunch of strangers. I started to cry. "I don't want to go," I said. "I want to stay here with you."

Annabel gave a gay little tinkle of a laugh, appropriate for when your adorable child says something adorable. "Lizzybit, I'm going to miss you too! But don't you want to see Grandma? Grandma would be so sad if you didn't go see her like you promised. And you'll be back home soon, right?"

Would I? This was news to me. Nobody had said how long I'd be gone – I thought I might be going to live with Grandma until I was grown. I nodded and wiped my snotty nose with the back of my hand, tears still flowing.

"We'll be boarding in a minute," said a second attendant to my mother. To me: "And you get to be first on the plane today!"

"Okay, Lizzybit!" She leaned over to give me one last hug, and I pressed my wet face against her belly. I lived in there once; I wanted to go back there now. "Okay, Bethie Beth. I gotta let you go now."

As though she were the one who didn't want to let go. She disentangled herself, smiling sweetly, blotches of my tears darkening spots on her wine-colored blouse.

The second attendant reached out towards me. "Beth, we have an activity pack just for you! Let's go down this hallway and we'll get it."

I nodded. She took my hand and began leading me towards the door to the boarding ramp. I turned back to take one last look at my mother, who was smiling and waving bye-bye.

"Love you," she called.

───────────

I had not seen my Grandma Doreen in nearly three years, but when the flight attendant escorted me to the meeting area, she was much as I'd remembered her: the neat silver-blonde cap of hair, the fake pearl earrings, the coral cardigan and white pants and freckled arms held at angles like a fortune cookie. She was smiling and blinking too much and waving tentatively, like she was asking a waiter for the check from across the restaurant.

"Hello, Elizabeth!" She opened her arms to me, and I hugged her around her waist. She smelled like rayon and sunscreen and coffee. I felt hungry and exhausted and grateful and bereft and a few other things, but mostly very, very happy to be hugging a person who was going to take care of me.

"Hi Grandma."

My transfer from flight attendant to Grandma was effected, my luggage collected, and a taxi was contracted to take us to Grandma's house in Clearwater. Grandma didn't live in the old house with the pool anymore, not since Grandpa Joe died of a stroke ("Stroke of *luck*," gloated Annabel) the year before, at the tender age of sixty-five. Since then, Grandma had moved to Clearwater, "...Where I'd always wanted to live," she told me, as we were driven past too many things for me to be able to process right then, all of them very brightly sunlit.

Grandma didn't seem to grieve for Grandpa Joe any more than my mother did. I barely remembered the guy, who was mostly uninterested in me when we lived there; I do however have several memories of him coming out of the bathroom naked, his penis like an upside-down fire hydrant, resulting in an irrational fear of firefighters that lasted well into my teens.

I knew Annabel hated her father, but I didn't know why, or even how. To me, it seemed like a life-threatening risk to hate one's parent – what did you have, if you didn't have your parent? I would be terrified to hate Annabel; even if I could have mustered the guts to feel that way, I would have squashed it inside. I had to love my mother, or she would never love me.

Grandma pointed out landmarks as we passed them. I was getting drowsy. I slumped against her side in exactly the way Annabel disliked most ("Watch it, you're crushing my ribs."). Grandma shifted and put one arm around me and sort of pet me on the upper arm for the rest of the ride home.

My time in Florida would not be wasted. On Monday, I was to be enrolled in my second third grade; I would also be enrolled in the after-school gymnastics program, for no fathomable reason, as I had neither athletic ability nor inclination. We would go to the store tomorrow to buy school supplies to replace the ones that had been left in my hastily vacated desk in New Jersey.

Grandma chattered about these plans, and the many day trips we'd take, and where we would go out for lunch sometime, as we installed my suitcases in her powder blue guest room. She took me around the "complex" to meet her neighbors, a bunch of sixtyish crepe-skinned women in floral capris who had a lot of time off to sit around the pool and play cards and talk about each other: Margery, Maddie, Maureen, Jeanette, and Riva. They made a gratifying amount of fuss over me.

"How long is she here for?" Riva asked. Her accent made it sound like "hee faw."

"Well, we're not quite sure," said Grandma Doreen. She ducked her head and patted her hair and looked away.

Should Riva have asked me, I would have answered, "For the rest of my life." I had already taken my shoes and socks off and rolled up my pants and was dangling my feet into the pool. One of the M's was running to her apartment to get some lemonade and cookies. Another told me I looked just like that little girl on that show, that one girl on that one show that everybody likes, the one with the family. "Adorable," the rest of them agreed.

By the time we'd headed back to Grandma's apartment, I was ebullient. Now I was the one who chattered, while she looked like she needed a nap: "Can I get new books? I wanted to bring my books from home, but I read them all anyway. I even read some of my mom's. There was one about a baby, but it was born, like, evil, and it killed people even though it was a baby. And this other one where a girl, she died in a fire, and then she came back to life, but nobody knew it was her..."

"Goodness," said Grandma, lashes fluttering. She patted her hair again and smoothed the unwrinkled polyester of her slacks.

"...And I read *A Little Princess*. I read it probably three times. And..."

"You must have had a lot of time to read at your mom's."

I knew I was becoming what Annabel termed "hyper," a state she abhorred, but I couldn't help it. I couldn't keep my voice from getting loud and urgent, couldn't stop wanting to fling myself across the room and burrow directly into my grandmother's lap. I jumped up and down for emphasis, talking about my books.

"I did! Because they would always send me to my room! And they'd say, 'Don't come out!' Even when I didn't do anything!"

I hoped Grandma could see how poorly treated I'd been at home. I hoped she might even be moved to call Annabel and tell her, "You were wrong about everything! You should be nicer to Beth and not ignore her!" I hoped Grandma felt sorry for me because of what I'd suffered, and wanted to make sure I was happy from now on to make up for it.

Certainly, my grandmother meant to do all of that. As soon as she stopped pinching the bridge of her nose like she wanted to stop smelling everything for all time. In the meantime, I could tell her eleven hundred thousand more things about how mean they were, but she raised her hand to stop me.

"Honey, can you please go into the bathroom medicine cabinet and get Grandma's aspirin?"

"Yes!" I cried, and sprang from my chair. I was an excellent aspirin-getter. "Do you want aspirin, acetaminophen, or ibuprofen?"

My grandmother looked up at me and smiled and blinked seventy times. "Just bring the orange bottle with the white cap. Thank you, dear."

———————

If I am going to blame Annabel for the way I am, I suppose I have to blame Grandma Doreen for the way Annabel is.

Doreen was a neurasthenic woman, subject to headaches and tired spells, discomfited by excessive noise or activity. She could never look you in the eye without blinking, literally closing her eyes until yours went away. With all her smiling and pants-smoothing and hair-touching, she was obviously hiding something. *Diazepam*, as the label on the orange bottle read, wasn't even the half of it.

What was she hiding? What caused her to live her life as one extended equivocation? I wonder if she even knew what it was, why she was so afraid all the time. She was terrified of her own daughter, I could hear it any time Annabel had her on the phone, and my mother's lifelong hurt and anger started to make more sense to me – I knew what it felt like to be feared by the woman who made you. Trying to talk to Doreen while she dodged and cringed and nattered off-topic at you was maddening; you just wanted to shake her and say, "For Christ's sake, I'm not going to hurt you!"

She tried, though; she tried so hard with me. She wanted to love me. She wanted to feel about me the way she spoke about me: proud of her granddaughter's precocious intelligence, happy to have a bright little companion around the house. She didn't want to fear me, and she didn't want to give up on me, and she could be as stubborn as the rest of us Madigan women, which turned out to be my salvation. No matter how I tested her patience, she told Annabel over the phone, "She's doing very well, dear. Everything is very well."

Part of it must have been spite. She took me in to appease my mother, but she also did it to prove that she was a good caretaker, to refute my mother's unspoken yet deafening claim that she had failed. If Doreen could take care of me, she could demonstrate her maternal fitness while making reparations for the worst of the damage her daughter had done.

I couldn't have articulated any of this back then, but I did feel it, and there was a deep sense of security in knowing that Grandma was not going to give up on me. She wasn't going to agree with my mother that I was the problem. The week I swallowed three pieces of chalk to thwart our teacher from progressing with class, Grandma told my mother, "She had a stomachache for a day or two, but she's feeling much better now." The week I told an elderly couple at the complex pool that my mommy had died in a robbery, and they turned up at Doreen's door the next day with tearful faces and a sympathy orchid, she told Annabel, "She talks about you quite a bit. When are you coming to visit her?"

She wasn't lying, exactly. She was covering. Something I learned from my grandmother: you don't always have to create a falsehood from whole cloth to lie. Sometimes you can draw the curtains over the truth. Sometimes you don't have to say anything at all.

———————

One thing I did not learn from my grandmother: anything about my father.

It was only in the past two years that I'd become curious about him, or the lack of him. For the first six years of my life, any questions I might have thought to ask were fobbed off with, "Not everybody has a daddy, sweetie," but as I learned more specifics about the mechanics of procreation, I started demanding to know which male person in particular had put his thing in mommy's thing and made her have a baby.

"We don't know," Annabel told me. The "we" made it sound like there was a team of scientists working on the problem. All follow-up questions received the same non-answer:

"Why don't we know?"

"Because we don't know."

Grandma Doreen was similarly unhelpful. When I asked her who or where my daddy was, she said, "Oh, honey, I can't answer that."

"Why?"

"Well, we're not sure."

"Why?"

"Honey, you'd have to ask your mom. I just don't know."

Blink blink blink blink blink. My grandmother was hiding a secret from me. Who was she protecting? Annabel? Herself? Me? Maybe she didn't want me to know who my father was because he was a bad person. Maybe he had hurt somebody and he was in jail.

I snooped for clues wherever I could, gingerly opening the crackling pages of the photo album I'd claimed from the high bookshelf in the living room. The pictures showed my mother throughout the ages: a toddler in a tub, a little girl with no front teeth on a bike, the annual school pictures, high school graduation. Then nothing for a while, then a very pregnant Annabel, and right after that, a picture of me, two or three months old, looking astonished and delighted to be alive and to be regarded. No father in sight.

"Poor thing," I overheard Margery saying to the other gals one afternoon. "No father." I was in the pool, practicing my spastic crawl, and was resting briefly before the next lap; they must not have seen me there, pressed against the pool wall. I only heard those four words before the subject changed, but that was enough to introduce the idea: I was an object of pity because I had no dad.

From then on, my missing father was a weapon with which to bludgeon anyone in my way. When my teacher reprimanded me for drawing hearts on the sole of my sneaker rather than practicing my times tables, I let my eyes fill with tears and said, "I drew them for my daddy, who went away." When the snotty girls in the popular group didn't want to trade stickers with me, I cried to the nearest adult, "They said they don't like me because I don't have a daddy." When I was caught trying to palm a pack of Life Savers at the stationery store while Grandma was talking to a friend outside, I looked at the mean owner lady who confronted me, burst into sobs, and said, "I don't have a daddy."

He was my Get Out of Jail Free card. He was my Boardwalk and my Park Place, the most valuable property I owned; he was my Reading Railroad and my Water Works. He was my green house, my red hotel, my pink paper money in the bank. I still wanted to know who he was, still fantasized that he was someone rich and famous, still hoped he would appear one day and tell me I could come live in his mansion and never have to do anything I didn't want to do ever again.

In the meantime, he was more useful to me in his absence.

———

I was happy at my Grandma's, as happy as I'd ever been. After school, the bus dropped me off at the complex, where she waited with an after-school snack of fruit salad, the canned old-people kind, with the sweet, metallic syrup. She looked at the tests I brought home, 98's and 100's circled in pen, marveling at my scholastic aptitude. If she had to go to the store or the bank or something, I would get in the beige Toyota and accompany her; if not, I might go down to the pool with her and read or swim while she played cards with the girls. If it rained, we'd stay inside and watch afternoon television, cozy under an afghan in the darkening room as the programs changed from old sitcoms to judge shows to local news.

I made my grandmother happy too, or so I hoped. I knew I was overwhelming – I knew I hugged her too hard, I saw her cringe when my volume rose too high – and I tried to tone it down, but I was just as overwhelmed by me as everyone else was. I was an inveterate leg swinger, chair kicker, plate dropper, public nuisance; she was always fielding the fallout from one of my antics. ("Beth is intentionally failing her school hearing test and claiming to be deaf.") But Grandma always forgave me – really forgave me. She knew none of this was my fault. She knew I loved her and I wanted to be good.

She is the only one who's ever known that about me.

I even had some school friends. There was nobody like Lillian, and there never would be again, but there were a few girls I could boss around pretty well. Not the princess girls; they were impenetrable to me, which was infuriating and fascinating in equal measure. They were just so outright *mean* all the time. And they acted so superior, even though other people were demonstrably smarter than them, and they didn't even care that they were dumb. They were vapid and obtuse on purpose, as was their argument for everything: "I know you are, but what am I?"

So I stuck to the more boring and marginal girls, inasmuch as I could stand them. I attended a pizza party for someone's birthday, got invited to play at a house or two. I even played the naked game a few times, and after our clothes went back on, I went through my new friend's bookshelves to see if there was anything good for me to borrow and not return.

Annabel still called regularly, but I didn't run to the phone the way I once had. Why would I? She'd sent me away. I was Grandma's girl now. And I know it pleased Doreen to get back on the phone, after I'd rushed through a perfunctory conversation with my mother, and say, "Of course she loves you, she just hasn't seen you in a while."

Then my mother's irate accusations, feeble and faraway through the filter of the phone, then Grandma again: "I'm not turning her against you, Annabel. She loves you as much as she ever has."

Oh, Doreen. I should have studied more of her science when I had the chance. I like to think I've incorporated some of her lessons – the power of denial, the pretense of not hearing things, saying "mmm," instead of "yes" or "no." But I am too angry and impatient, too much my rapacious mother's daughter, to truly follow my grandmother's graceful way-of-no-way, the babbling brook that bends itself around rocks and erodes them bit by bit. *She loves you as much as she ever has*, indeed.

———————————

Then the cancer started.

It started first with Kath, a friend of Jeanette's, who was diagnosed with (lowered voices) stage three metastatic breast cancer. I sat on a chaise near their table with a book on my lap and eavesdropped on the ladies as they discussed it:

"I can't even imagine."

"Of course you can! After Margery's sister last year? Same thing. It starts in the breast and then it spreads."

"The poor woman. Does she have anybody?"

"Well, she's got the one daughter, but she's in Michigan..."

"Uccchhh..."

"...I know!"

"I'm worried about her. I really am."

In my four months in Florida, I had never heard the gals so serious, so reverent, as when they talked about Kath's cancer. Suddenly every conversation was about who had had cancer, what stage, where it started, how it ended: "Pancreatic. Very bad." "Ovarian. She did the chemo three times. It didn't work." "She was in remission for five years and then bam."

Cancer. It was the most important overriding circumstance in the world. It was the worst thing that could possibly happen to you that didn't involve your immediate death. There was no joking around about it; usually when the group got serious, someone changed the subject to something funny. With cancer, they let their voices trail off, looked at their hands, and sighed.

Then someone tried to abduct one of the second graders who went to my school, and everybody got even more grave. A policeman came to our class to tell us what to do if a stranger came up to you: You shouldn't talk to a stranger, even if he or she offers you candy, or says they know your mother, and you should *never* get into a car with somebody you don't know.

Okay, no problem. But why did anybody try to take Tyler McKenzie away in a car in the first place? Most of the adults I knew wanted fewer children, not more of them. The policeman's answer was vague, like Grandma when she was holding back: "Well, sometimes people have a disease in their minds, and the disease makes it so they don't know what's right or wrong, and they might have a bad idea..."

It was May, and the already thick air of central Florida thickened further with mounting public anxiety. Parents were picking their kids up right after school; no playground time, no after-school guests. The mood by the pool was gloomy. I used to be able to get an obligatory two minutes of doting from the gals before they wanted to talk about grown-up things; now they had only quick, flat smiles and *that's nice, dear*'s for me, before they went back to prognosticating death by cancer for everyone in sight.

Grandma was taking more naps, and more "aspirin." It was my

fault; I knew it. Not a week went by without a note or a phone call from school: "Beth is refusing to participate in the Pledge of Allegiance." "Beth is claiming to be her 'twin sister,' Lilith." "Beth has been telling her classmates that she can command her grandfather's ghost to kill people in their sleep."

Doreen "mmm"-ed as strenuously as she could, blinking like she was staring into the sun, as one neighbor stopped by to complain that I stole her catalogs, another that I kept meowing at her dachshunds. But maintaining the necessary level of denial was becoming physically impossible for her.

I mean, she was sixty-two – and I know that's the new forty-two, or whatever, but she'd already been through so much in her life: all the "mmm"-ing she'd had to do over Annabel, the thirty-eight year marriage to Grandpa Joe ("Not the easiest man – he and your mother had a lot of differences – you both take after him in some ways – miss him? mmm, of course, mmm") and then when her bitchy daughter finally leaves and her difficult husband finally dies, she gets saddled with this insane tornado child, a girl nobody thus far had ever been able to love.

Of course it was taking a toll on her. God knew, it was taking a toll on me. It wasn't easy being me, perpetually having to come up with new reasons that everybody should like me, or feel sorry for me, or at least notice me. Tyler McKenzie had raised the stakes so high – *everybody* treated him deferentially now, kids and adults, and why? Because he was an idiot who was about to climb in some stranger's car before a passerby spooked the driver? How did that make him worthy of notice? Why was that an achievement?

How come *I* couldn't get nearly abducted?

Why couldn't *I* have cancer?

And really, why *couldn't* I have cancer? I could've had it and not known it; a lot of the gals' stories involved people with mysterious symptoms that they thought were nothing until they went to the doctor and wham! Cancer. Turned out they only had three months to live.

I often felt like I was dying. There were times when, out of nowhere, my heart beat wrong, my eyesight froze, my breath was too far away, and I felt like I was being rushed away from the rest of the world. Other times I wanted to rip my body apart before I burst from the inside. The nothing-matters feeling I got when I made myself faint started to come over me unprovoked, sitting on the bus after school, or watching Grandma fall asleep on the sofa, and I'd have trouble figuring it out: I was dreaming, no I wasn't, this was real, what is real, who was this voice that was thinking these things, these two voices, and did they prove my existence or negate it?

I definitely had cancer. No, but really this time.

There's a common liars' superstition: If you say it, you are asking it to come true. Sometimes you want that to happen: You met a famous person and they adored you and you're best friends now. But if you try to get out of a social engagement by claiming that your cat is sick, you might as well kill your cat right now, because you've lied that outcome into existence.

Therefore, my decision to have cancer made it that much more plausible in my mind that I actually did or would have cancer, which then made me terrified that I had done something fatal I couldn't undo, and the terror meant that I didn't actually want cancer, so I had no reason to lie and say I did, which gave me the conviction I needed to truly believe it.

I began my cancer journey by confronting my imminent death.

I am going to die, I told myself. I am dying, and nothing can save me.

Good. The shiver, the ache in the solar plexus – palpable. This is how emotion is transmuted into energy, a thought becomes a force. I continued with momentum.

And after I'm dead, there won't be a 'me' anymore. I won't exist, and I won't even know it. All my thoughts and memories will disappear. It will be like I was never here at all. I'll never get to do anything for the rest of eternity except be dead.

Better. This was legitimately terrifying. Some people were afraid of Hell, where you suffered forever because of all the bad things you did. As an atheist, I didn't need Hell to be afraid – I had eternal consciousless nothingness to fear. Hell might hurt, but at least you would exist.

In this fatalistic frame of mind, wherein I really did believe that I was hosting a killer cancer that would imminently be discovered and diagnosed by doctors, there was no time to waste. Everybody should know about it right away, so I'd be able to enjoy some of the attention before I died.

I went to school the next day and announced it to the girl I considered my closest friend: a bland girl named Cassandra who had at least read all the Narnia books and would sometimes pretend to be witches with me. I caught her out in the hallway by the water fountain before class started and showed her the two vitamin pills ("Active Seniors Formula") I'd taken from the bottle on the counter at home.

"I have to take these pills because I have cancer," I told her. I tucked my chin and opened my eyes wide and tried to look very sick. "It's a secret. Don't tell anybody."

"No you don't," scoffed Cassandra. "You don't have cancer."

My eyes opened wider – how dare she not believe me! Did she not see how sick I looked? Did she not see my cancer pills? "Yes I do! I don't want anybody to know."

Cassandra regarded me with narrowed eyes, scanning me for cancer, finding me wanting. Her nose wrinkled, like, *What is wrong with you? Wait, you know what – I don't even want to know.*

This was from Cassandra, who picked her nose and swallowed her gum and didn't even remember what a warlock was; Cassandra, who thought being goalie in soccer made her goalie of the entire world; Cassandra, upon whom I'd bestowed the favor of my friendship despite her shitty, subpar personality.

"The *doctor* told me," I said, appalled and self-righteous. "I could *die.*"

"No he didn't."

Cassandra turned away and opened the classroom door. I grabbed her arm to stop her from walking through it. "Yes he did!"

She tried to wrest away, whining, playing it up for attention. "Ow! Stop it!"

"*You* stop it!"

"Ms. Sussman, Beth is lying!" yelled Cassandra. "And she's hurting me!"

"No I'm not!"

I wanted to hurt her, though, and if she didn't stop talking right away and take everything back and reset the day to before this all went wrong, I would kill her with my bare hands and my bare teeth while kicking her to death, I really would. It was coming. It was imminent. It had already happened, so it couldn't be stopped.

It was time to faint. I took in the deepest breath I could, and held it until my hand slipped from Cassandra's arm and the noise around me dimmed.

Then I fell.

PART II

BETTY

2002

[4]

Psych

Was it an honest suicide attempt that landed me here? Of course
it was. Any attempt is an honest one, even the ones for show.
If you're desperate enough to be faking suicide, either you're
legitimately suicidal or you should be.

It's not that I didn't want to kill myself; I did. How else to stop
the pain? What better way to punish the people who'd hurt me?
But I kept getting stuck on the "being dead" part. I *wanted* to
want to kill myself, but I was too chickenshit to commit.

I prayed for the strength to kill myself many times, ever since
I was twelve years old, but I'm too weak. I've castigated myself,
hated myself, hit myself, cut myself, but I never killed myself. I
"tried" – but what did I try? I tried *not* to kill myself while trying
to kill myself.

And that's harder than you might think. Take it from me:
You might have your staged attempt all planned out, but when
you're sitting on the edge of the tub with the pills and the knife,
you hold your life in your hands. There's always the risk, when
you start fucking around with pills and knives, that you might
succeed in spite of yourself, or wind up brain damaged but alive,
worse off than you were and unable to finish the job.

Any attempt to harm your body is honest. You pay for it
with pain. You can't barter or borrow it away, you can't hire
somebody to take it for you. Nobody else takes that pain but

you. Someone should remind the paramedics, the nurses, the cops: No matter the source, the pain is real.

You want incentive to kill yourself? Be a seventeen-year-old girl who swallows too many pills but not quite enough, who cuts yourself too hard but misses all the veins. Look at the apathy in the eyes of the person who loads you onto the stretcher – you can't, because they won't look at you. That's how boring you are. Everybody in the ER is shaking their heads. You're another worthless brat wasting their time; they could be helping people who need it. Questions are put to you in a monotone, smiles are intentionally flat.

Try to kill yourself and fail, and you will damn sure be motivated to get it right the next time.

My roommate's name is Courtney. She's a cutter.

Courtney is fifteen. She has been cutting since she was twelve. Cutting on its own is not impressive, unless, like Courtney, you cut the wrong spot one day, and leave nearly two pints of blood all over the bathroom before the paramedics arrive. I don't think Courtney's going to be here very long; you can tell how serious she is about getting better and going home. Accidentally slicing open your ulnar artery will scare a bitch straight.

Most of us on the unit bear cutting scars. Some girls' are on their inner thighs; you can't see them unless they show you. Mine are right there on my left shoulder, twenty-five or thirty of them, a patch of horizontal lines like I scribbled on myself to scratch out something underneath. I like to pet them, when possible; when the weather is warm enough for me to wear short sleeves, I'll spend most of the day with my right arm across my chest, strumming my fingertips over my scars. When it's cold, I keep my hand there and press against the fabric of my shirt.

We're not supposed to fetishize our damage. No "war stories" in group, no graphic descriptions of self-harm. So my sensuous enjoyment of my scars is provocative, I know, but it's both self-soothing *and* aggravating to others, so I love doing it twice as much.

Maureen is facilitating group today. Maureen is in her late twenties, she is humorless, and she has what I judge to be unjustifiably abundant self-esteem. She is my least favorite of all the counselors; I sincerely hope that I am her least favorite patient. She sees me arm-fondling and turns the group's focus to me.

"Is something making you anxious today, Betty?"

"Just life," I say quickly, dropping my hand from my scars. "Just everything."

Oppositional, like it says in my file. Unwilling to participate in the therapy process. Progress has been minimal; will continue to be minimal unless patient develops trust and relational skills and engages in meaningful exploration of her issues. But let's be honest – that's not happening anytime soon. I'm enjoying it here, and I'm not ready to leave.

Maureen's face, for instance. It reminds me of my mother, the look of someone who can't stand you and isn't allowed to admit it. How challenging to a woman like Maureen, who wants to help troubled kids and make a difference in the world because she believes that's her calling. She is meant to *save lives*. Like, *her entire identity* is dependent on her being this morally righteous figure of benevolence and wisdom who works miracles with last-chance teens. And then there's me. And she wants to wring my neck.

She's nodding at me, serious look on her flat, wide face. What a fake fucking idiot. "So, pretty much everything is making you anxious today."

"Everything, every day," I say defiantly. Because I am a classic case of Oppositional Defiant Disorder, Code 313.81 in the Diagnostic and Statistical Manual of Mental Disorders. I challenge authority, I am non-compliant, I argue all the time for the fun of it, I blame others for my actions, I am resentful and vindictive, et cetera. Right on the cusp of Conduct Disorder (312.8); not yet Antisocial Personality Disorder (301.7).

"So where is that fear located in your body?"

I cross my legs tighter, pull my arms closer around my chest, tuck my chin. I remember being eight years old and alone in the garage with my best friend Lillian's older brother: the dank air, the salt of his fingers inside me, the depth of my shame. I suppress the urge to twitch. *Take a guess, Maureen. Where do you think the fear is located?*

"It's not in my body," I say resentfully to my lap. "It's in my mind."

Maureen leans forward, oozing self-congratulation. She's got me talking, when usually I just sass off and refuse to speak; she's *engaging* me. I can see her going home and telling her boyfriend (or, more likely, her parents) how she eked a sentence or two from that hard case today. "Okay, and what do you mean by that? What do you think the difference is?"

Now, see, if Maureen wanted to have an actual discussion of the mind-body problem, I would be totally into that. As someone who has had to overcome the body's built-in impulse to protect itself in order to do the mind's bidding, I have developed several salient thoughts on the issue, and I'll bet the rest of the gals have too. But we can't talk about anything interesting; that would take away from the hours and hours we need to talk about our feeeeeeeeeeelings.

"One is my body, and the other one is the thing in my skull."

I'm such a snotty brat. Nicole the Borderline Personality (301.5) smirks at me from across the circle: *Good one.* It's not all that good, but Nicole has very low standards, as do most of the nitwits in here. They're the ones I feel sorry for, honestly; they have nothing to go home to when this is over. This is the most explicit and sustained psychological care they'll ever receive. This bullshit will be the high point of their emotional lives.

"So," says Maureen, as though we're having a conversation. "Whatever it is, it makes you too anxious to even talk about it. But you're talking to yourself about it, aren't you."

Wow. I look momentarily alarmed, caught in the act, because what she said was so *true*. I can refuse to talk about what happened to me, but it will always have happened. Wow, Maureen. That's so super apt. I've never thought of it that way before. You should write a book. I nod briefly, eyes down, and she knows she must be breaking through to me, because as hard-assed as I try to be, right now I look like the young girl I was in that garage: vulnerable, scared, and in pain.

Her voice softens. She won't push me too hard too fast, the way another counselor might; she's savvier than that. "Will you think about what you might need to say, and we'll come back to you?"

I scowl and shake my head no – back to oppositional and defiant. Maureen moves on to Ophira. I don't know what the DSM code is for Ophira. There may not be a code for Spoiled Idiot Whose Very Wealthy but Emotionally Inconsistent Parents Left Her with No Internal Resources. Ophira's storyline is so predictable and dull; if I could somehow unfollow her in person, I would.

I stay perfectly still and work on making myself cry. The group may shift its focus wherever it likes, but in about three minutes, one by one, they're going to notice me silently crying. And no matter what anybody else is saying, no matter what kind of excruciating memory they're recovering or critical breakthrough they're having, it won't matter. My noiseless tears will drown them out.

I'll get bored with this place eventually; I always do. But right now I don't mind taking a vacation from Out There. It takes its toll on you, living the way I do. I need to rest sometimes if I'm going to perform at my best. Right now, for several reasons, this is the most expedient place for me to be.

Many people will tell you they have a "thing" about hospitals. Ask your average American to visit someone in the hospital, and six out of ten will beg off, citing a "thing" they have. "Oh, sorry, hospitals freak me out." "I'm one of those people who hates hospitals." (These are the same people who announce that they're "the type" who "hate funerals," or "hate waiting in line," as though most other people just *love* grief and frustration.)

My "thing" about hospitals is the opposite: You can't keep me away from them.

I was always fascinated by the hospital, even before my diagnosis at age nine. Here was a place where the air was charged with immediacy and purpose, a place where spare human parts – blood, plasma, organs – were exchanged and replaced, where life could be dismantled and rebuilt. It was the physical portal between being and not-being, a kind of existential purgatory. The rest of the world drove itself crazy trying to ignore the realities of suffering and death. In the hospital, they were the only things that mattered.

URGENT CARE, said the signs. That's what I'd been looking for my whole life.

My cancer started with a lump in my throat. As a child of neglect, I had one of those pretty much all the time, so I didn't notice anything different at first. It was a piece of something I couldn't keep down and couldn't cough up, lodged in there like a gumball stuck in a machine. It hurt every time I tried to swallow, especially when I tried to swallow my words.

So nobody noticed my new lump until I was seen wincing when I tried to eat. My mother took me to the doctor, and the doctor said, as soon as she palpated the lump, "Yeah, we're going to want to biopsy this."

Within two weeks, the word came down: Pediatric papillary thyroidal cancer. The thyroid had to come out, the radiation had to go in. The prognosis in this kind of cancer was good, if it hadn't metastasized yet, but nothing was guaranteed. Even if I beat it the first time, I would spend the rest of my life anticipating remission.

I was out of it for so much of the ordeal, it's hard for me to remember exactly what happened exactly when. I know I had my first surgery, the lobectomy, at the Cornell Medical Center, up on 69th Street in Manhattan, just a few blocks from my parents' apartment; I remember I was terrified beforehand that something would go wrong during the operation. I was afraid that I might die, or even worse, I might live and lose the ability to talk.

When I woke up in the recovery room, my mother tells me I said, "Am I alive? Can I talk?" And when I'd been assured of those things, I fell into a deep, relieved sleep.

The second surgery came only weeks later: My cancer had metastasized; they had to go back in for some lymph nodes. The recovery from this one was much harder than the first – a bigger incision, necessitating a tube stuck into the wound to drain it, plus significant pain while I tried to regain my full range of motion. I'd only spent a few nights in the hospital the first time, but this stay was at least two weeks.

For most of that time, I had the same roommate, a six-year-old girl named Riva whose too-large brown eyes were the only spots of color on her pale face. She wore a turban of white gauze that hid her surgical scars. Riva and I talked often from our respective beds; early on, she told me in her high, wispy voice how she came to the hospital "by mistake."

"Mommy said if I was good at the doctor, I could get to ride in th' ambulance, and I'd go around and around and I could make the siren go." Tears bloomed in her eyes. "She said I could come back home after. I want to go home."

"You're going to go home soon," I assured her. "And then I'll miss you."

A few days before my discharge, I was taken for a routine scan. There were a bunch of other patients waiting ahead of me, and it took longer than it should have. When I got back to the room, Riva was gone. She'd had a seizure and coded. Her little body was already on its way to the morgue. I collapsed into my bed, weeping with grief. How could this have happened? It was impossible. She was just there an hour ago, talking about what she was going to do when she got home; I could still hear her teeny-tiny voice in my head. "Beddy, I'ma visit you when I'm home 'n then you won't miss me."

Riva, I'm glad you are home now. And I will always miss you.

Then there was the radiation and the chemo: the unremitting nausea, the dizziness and fatigue, the hair loss. At the worst of it, I weighed sixty pounds. I looked like the ghost of a lollipop in a bad wig. I didn't allow anybody to take my picture for the entire year.

Here's what I remember most: the loneliness of my dark bed at home in the daytime, the panicked sense of being watched by the empty room. The nightmares where some malevolence had invaded my body, and I couldn't yell for help – I'd wake up croaking, trying to scream. Beat-up issues of incongruous magazines in inevitable waiting rooms: Popular Aviation, Black Entrepreneur. Endless popsicles. Ginger ale burps. Puking through my mouth and nose at the same time. Puking hard enough to break a rib.

When I was finally ready to go back to school, I'd missed most of the year. It didn't matter; I still tested above grade level, and I was allowed to resume my place in the fourth grade three weeks before summer would begin. The other kids, who I'd barely known before my abrupt withdrawal, saw the scar at the bottom of my throat and called me Frankenstein.

You can barely see the scar any more, it's so old. Now it just looks like the faintest scratch from a nail scissor, less than a half inch long. I still get screened for recurrence twice a year; I still pray each time. I have remained cancer free so far, but you never know.

———

For someone as fucked up as me, therapy is like ping pong. It's therapeutic in that it's a diverting game, requiring attention and competitive focus; it's enjoyable to the extent that one can score on one's opponent. But ultimately it's pointless. Some days you don't feel like playing.

I'd rather be reading a book. It was a long morning. I woke up early and couldn't get back to sleep. I was in that agitated state of mind where you can't stop thinking about some situation that makes you want to kill yourself – like, "honestly" want to kill yourself. That state where you'd give anything to be able to shut off the thoughts, and you can't, and you're thinking, "I want to stop thinking about this, please let me stop thinking about this," and the sense of being trapped and helpless mounts, and it's *so* gruesome and *so* grueling, and there's nothing but *more gruel* on the menu, every goddamn meal, bowls and bowls of it, a steaming pile of the laxative, stomach-turning groats of regret and shame, served with a poison spoon that's on fire.

It's not about what you'd think. It's not my friend's brother in the garage. It's not what happened freshman year, or what happened with Grandpa Joe. It's not the earliest or the worst instance of abuse in my life. It's not even the most recent. It's so stupid; I would never talk about it with any of the counselors or therapists here.

We have individual therapy after lunch. First there's morning chores, then breakfast, then house meeting, then we break up into groups, we do that whole thing for ninety minutes, and then maybe I have a half-hour to myself before lunch, and then Dinah. So by the time I get there, I'm spent. That's part of their plan, I'm sure; they wear you down all morning, then they get you alone when you're groggy from lunch, and use your exhaustion as a truth serum.

Today I have manifested many typical behaviors: I was distracted during meeting and group, I was disinclined to talk, I appeared to be hiding something. All true.

"You seem...subdued today," says Dinah.

Dinah's not a bad sort. I didn't find myself drawn to her at first; she's too old. I like mine on the younger, idealistic side. She's like forty-five, short, wizened and nasally, which makes her very easy to mock; anything you say in that Dinah-voice is going to sound ridiculous. But she's wry, and there's something about Dinah's brand of cognitive behaviorism that doesn't smack as completely of futility as everyone else's. She's not sentimental or overly familiar, and she doesn't pretend she knows you better than you know yourself, the way the rest of them do. When we talk, I can see the point she's driving at. She's probably not even that brilliant, in an IQ sense, but – how to put this? – she knows what it is that she wants to know.

What she wants to know is, what do you want? Not in that rhetorical, "Do you *want* to fail out of high school without a degree?" kind of way. She's honestly interested in what we want, I think. And sometimes I feel like honestly responding: I want to be loved unconditionally and taken care of for the rest of my life by every single person I meet.

"Yeah, I feel subdued."

Dinah nods. "That's okay. You don't have to be dramatic to entertain me."

That's good. I don't have anything to say. I don't want to pick up where we left off on Friday. I don't want to talk about the weekend. The weekend was uneventful. I wrote some emails and updates to send and post when I have access to the internet again. As you might imagine, I have many pen pals.

I don't want to think about them either. So many complications. It's good – it's good that I'm in here right now, it's good that I can't get online. It's better this way. It's for my own protection. I am protected here.

I'm tired.

"I don't feel bad, per se," I tell her. "It's more like, weary."

"Tired," she says. "But not too, too unhappy."

"Yeah, not the worst. Not the lowest of the low."

I'm oddly calm. Suddenly everything seems manageable: I'll just stay in this chair in this office for the rest of my life. What was I so worried about at five this morning? This happens sometimes – as miserable as I am at five in the morning, I am equally incredulous at five in the afternoon that I was so miserable over something so unimportant. Then, twelve hours later, as I'm quaking in my bed in the darkest-before-dawn, I am even more incredulous at that blithe ninny of five p.m. yesterday, all *la la la la la, everything is fine*...and now I have to kill myself all over again.

I am incredulous. I am incredibly incredulous. I lack credulity. I have poor credit. Garage, garage, garage...

"I used to make myself faint when I was a kid," I say, apropos of nothing.

Dinah nods. "What was that like?"

I could tell her, too. She's curious. And she's kind of unflappable. *It was fantastic*, I could say. That's when I realized that my body was mine alone, only I could control it from the inside, it did whatever I wanted before I even formed the thought. That's how I first saw the simultaneous planes of existence, how the world changed according to my eyes, how the same classroom became slower as I was going down. It set me apart from others, this special skill; it was a thrill and a spectacle only I could provide.

Why did I tell Dinah about my fainting? I feel faint right now. "It's weird," I say. *Eerd eerd eerd.* "I'm not feeling well."

"Do you want to lie down? Have some water." Dinah reaches into the mini fridge by her chair, passes a bottle of water to me over her ottoman, piled with papers and magazines and files.

I have the feeling of writing everything down as it's happening, like I'm narrating all this from my chair: I hold the bottle of water in my left hand, use the palm of my right to turn the cap counterclockwise, the plastic resists and breaks. I remove the cap, lift the bottle, and drink. Dinah is watching me calmly and with interest. Am I talking out loud?

"Your ottoman is a desk," I tell her, testing what it sounds like to talk. Yeah, that part was out loud, but the rest was in my head. I'm good.

"So it is," she says. "But when I put my feet up on my desk, it evens out."

This isn't happening. How do I know this is happening? Maybe I'm imagining this. Dinah is tricking me. She knows something she shouldn't, she can read my mind. No, no. What's happening? I have to make sure she can't tell that I'm not okay.

"Ha ha ha," I say.

"Betty, are you sure you don't want to lie down?"

I'm not sure of anything. I shake my head. "I'm okay." But I'm not. I'm scared. I don't know how to act when I'm not acting. I feel like I might cry – really cry, though, uncontrollably. I wish I knew why. I don't know how long it's been since I honestly cried. Since I honestly did anything.

Is this dissociating? This is how it feels when I fake it. This happens a lot to survivors of sexual abuse, dissociation. I once read a book about a woman who developed multiple personalities because she was so badly abused as a child. She'd partitioned her consciousness so she didn't have to live with her reality; different parts spoke in different voices with different personalities, and they didn't know what the other ones were up to. The syndrome is called DID now, Dissociative Identity Disorder (300.14); there's some skepticism in the analytic community as to whether it's always fictitious or whether it's sometimes real. For myself, if I wanted to fake a disorder, I would go with Dissociative Fugue (300.13) – it's not as much fun as multiple personalities, but at least everyone agrees it exists.

Too much personality, that's my problem. Everyone agrees. All of us: the cancer girl and the compulsive cutter and scarredgrrl@hotmail.com and whoever it is sitting here in this chair in Dinah's office, nominally in charge of us all. Too much.

"Here," Dinah says, coming around to the back of my chair. "Let me help you."

She assists me in standing and moving the two feet backwards to her couch. I lay down gratefully, close our eyes, and hope our mouth will follow.

———————

Nota Bene: I mentioned "my parents" above – that's what I call my mother and her third husband, a man named Chip, as in, "to break off a small piece of something larger." I have never known my biological father. I don't even know who he is. After lo these seventeen years on Earth, I have become convinced that my mother doesn't know who he is either. If there were anybody else in the world who could be held responsible for me, she certainly would have named him.

As it is, she is stuck with me, and so is Chip. Fortunately, Chip makes a lot of money, which makes everybody that much happier and easier to get along with. Chip and his money paid for the finest care during my thyroid cancer; Chip's money sent me to a private school in Manhattan, and then to a boarding school in upstate New York; Chip's money is currently covering the whopping cost of inpatient psychiatric care that is not covered by Chip's insurance.

My mother, who goes by Anna ("Ahna"), was introduced to Chip by her second husband, Chuck. I missed much of the marriage to Chuck, as I was living in Florida with my grandparents that year, until the unfortunate thing with Grandpa Joe happened. Anna was married to Chuck when I left, and engaged to Chip by the time I got back.

"When I left," hah. When I was *sent away*. When I was a child, my mother sent me away to live with her parents, because I was inconvenient. What do you think about that, Maureen? I have no father, because my mother is careless – as in, she couldn't care less about who impregnated her. Then I have no mother either.

Then I have my grandparents: Grandpa Joe, with his early onset dementia, and Grandma Doreen, who took Xanax like they were multivitamins for active seniors. You can imagine how well that worked for everyone. Of course something untoward was going to happen, and of course it was going to happen to me. My mother knew that; how could she not have known? She knew her parents well enough to know that she didn't want to live anywhere near them. Me, though, her eight year old daughter – I'd be fine.

God, now I'm doing it – that thing where you whine forever about how your mother (Narcissistic Personality Disorder, 301.81) ruined your life. Pathetic. True, in my case, but still pathetic.

I'm not giving in; I'm not going to be one of these lumpy dumdums around the sharing circle, in the throes of their catharses, snuffling and glistening like baby pigs. I couldn't even if I wanted to.

But you can see why the hospital fetish, yes? The 24-7 attention; someone asking at least once per hour, "How do you feel?" Being told you're brave. Being referred to as "Honey." Having people look into your eyes. Hearing, "I'm sorry this hurts so much, Baby." "I'm gonna come back and check on you later, Sweetie." Jigsaw puzzles. Morning game shows. Endless popsicles. Being sponge-bathed, being fed, being tucked in every night. Being treated like a fucking child for once in one's life.

Since I was seven years old and falling off chairs, I knew the price of love was pain. If the price of being in the hospital was cancer, I was ready to pay with my life.

5

Frog Soup: An Experiment

Hypothesis: According to a gruesome, oft-told anecdote, a live frog, if placed in a pot of cool water on a stove, will not notice a very gradual rise in the temperature of that water, and will sit there placidly boiling to death without making a single move to save itself, as long as the temperature does not rise at a rate greater than 0.002 degrees centigrade per second, thereby providing us a useful metaphor for understanding human habituation and the disinclination to change.

Materials: Theoretical frog, theoretical pot, theoretical water, theoretical source of controllable heat, theoretical sadist willing to boil a live animal to death for sheer fuck of it. Actual human girl, age 10. Actual universe, age unknown.

Procedure:

Send human girl, fresh from ten months of battling pediatric papillary thyroidal cancer, to private school in Manhattan for the fifth grade. Her hair will be chopped a little too short, and she will have a small scar at the base of her throat, which she will touch nigh constantly. She will also have expensive clothes selected by her mother, who has graduated, as a newish resident of the Upper East Side, from the Paramus Park Mall to Saks Fifth Avenue. That's how much money Chip has.

Of course, Chip's money will be but peanuts, the humblest of all nuts, compared to some of her classmates, some of whom will be overheard imperiously asking people, "Do you know who my father is?" She should resist the urge to say sympathetically, "You don't know yours either?" They mean something different.

She can, however, take comfort in the fact that her stepfather may have only peanuts compared to some other fathers, both step and standard, but he has many millions of peanuts, due to his prescient personal investment in the tech sector, and that ain't peanuts. She will be neither the richest nor the poorest in her class, and she will be able to compete on the birthday party front, at least until she reaches thirteen, at which point the bat mitzvahs will take over and murder everyone.

Watch her try to make friends. Remember, it's been two years since she had any. She will lack the vocabulary of these Manhattan kids, who communicate mostly in syllables and acronyms. She can outread any of them, could do so blindfolded, and is willing to let people copy her homework or cheat off her test, but there are areas of knowledge she doesn't have: social intelligence, years of amassed pop culture trivia, picking the right things and people to like or dislike. Knowing when to quit.

Begin.

Stage One: Fifth grade

I didn't realize that ten-year-olds were different from old women in Florida. Kids are not nearly as interested in my cancer as they should be. My scar is too small and indistinct to be impressive, it just looks like a scratch, and my stories of suffering are unappealing. Even the heartrending tale of little Riva is met with puzzled looks, like, *Why are you telling us this?* My opening gambit thus wasted, I fall into a social limbo that lasts through November, when I begin to find a niche with some honor roll kids, if only through proximity.

I do well in class. I try to ingratiate myself to teachers. I almost always do better with adults than peers. This is depressing but better than nothing. Too bad so many of the younger teachers here are in thrall to the princes and princesses; they're pathetically obvious about wanting to be liked by the cool kids, which just feeds these kids' near-sociopathic sense of superiority and contempt. I seethe with resentment over this all day long.

But eventually I have become friendly with two separate girls: Paige, with whom I have advanced placement math after school on Mondays, and Erin, with whom I have advanced placement English after school on Wednesdays. I become friends with both of them the same way: walking to the bus after our late class, hanging out at their house for an hour or two here and there. Parallel relationships, like we study in both English and Math.

I am closer to Paige than I am to Erin. Erin has other friends. Paige doesn't really. I try to mix with Erin's friends and am tolerated but not embraced. One day I am bragging about all the things I have successfully shoplifted, and they all start wrinkling their noses. I clarify: I only did it because we used to be very poor. "That's tragic," says a girl named Heather Glazer.

Heather Glazer is the coolest girl in the group because she cares less than anybody else, also because she keeps the lift tickets from her family's ski vacations clipped to the zipper of her down coat; they're so much a part of her wardrobe, she forgets they're there. I would like to push her down the stairs.

But it doesn't matter, because over winter break, I meet a whole bunch of people at this program for kids who have survived cancer. It's like a circus thing where you get to swing from trapezes and jump on trampolines, and if that sounds dumb, you also get to ride jet skis and be in a fashion show. It's in Miami, and you have to have cancer to be part of it, that's probably why nobody's heard of it. I got a boyfriend while I was there. He's from France and his name is Laurent. I receive several letters from him, all written with the same thin, fine-tipped blue pen in a handwriting markedly different from my own.

Before Easter vacation, I invite a few people over to my house to watch movies and make sundaes. Paige comes, and Erin, and Erin's friends: Heather, Megan, Madison, Alyssa, and Dakota. They're in my house, but they're not being very nice to me. Dakota asks if I was bald when I had cancer, and if so, do I have any pictures? Megan is whispering to Alyssa in the corner while looking right at me. Madison asks, "Who's your real father again?" When my mother comes out of her room to say goodbye to my friends, Heather Glazer asks her, "Does Betty really have a boyfriend from France?"

Anna, to her everlasting credit, looks at Heather and says, "I'm sorry, which one are you...Heather? Mmm. Mm hmm."

After Easter vacation, I am given to understand that Paige is now friends with Erin *et al*, and though I got them together, they are now pursuing a friendship that does not include me. Like, ostentatiously doesn't include me. Sometimes I will still get to hang out with one of them alone after our advanced class, but they each spend most of the time talking about the other, sometimes in a good way, sometimes bad. If I agree with the bad, it gets back to the other right away.

They also like to cross-check things I've told them separately: "Didn't you tell Erin your father was dead? But you told me you don't know who he is."

A long pause, while I try to recover from visible alarm: "Because...I don't know who he is, so...he's dead to me."

The incredible internet machine in Chip's home office provides my only opportunity for much needed contact with like-minded individuals. Using my mother's America OnLine account, I am able to register "my daughter" for her own account, to verify that "my daughter" is over the age of thirteen, and to erase enough traces of said exchange that my mother has no understanding of what has transpired.

I begin several alternate lives. I am an orphan; I am a sexy teenage girl; I am a famous child actress who can't tell you my real name because if I did you'd treat me differently, the way everyone else does, and the internet is the only way I can have anything resembling a normal childhood.

In real life ("IRL," as we say on the internet), I am a goat. I'm not a nobody; I'm not ignored. I don't have to sit at the lunch table with the two exchange students and the weird, greasy girl and Duane, who's always in trouble. I can sit at the clique table, but if Erin and/or Paige is not there, I get a distinctly unwelcoming vibe from Madison, Alyssa, Dakota, Megan, and especially Heather. I may slide my tray onto the edge of their table, but I'll still be sitting by myself. Even when Paige and/ or Erin is there, I serve at their leisure: if they ask me to tell a particular story, I will, and if they then want to pick that story apart, they may.

I know I'm there as entertainment. But at least I'm there.

By May, I am counting the hours until the year is over. I recognize this from every other school I ever attended. I wish it didn't always go so exactly the same. I wish I could find a new way to be me. If I had another chance, I'd do everything differently – I know, but I *swear* it this time. I promise myself that over the summer I will find some way to never come back to this school again.

Findings: Frog reports that water was not exactly cool to begin with, it's heating up very rapidly, and she would dearly love to hop out of the pot, but there's a lid on it.

Stage Two: Sixth grade

More of the same. And still I never learn. I come back from summer with two more holes in each earlobe and one on the right cartilage, because I am punk rock now. I am the most punk rock eleven-year-old there is.

I did not manage to find a way to transfer to a new school over the summer, but I did go to a sleepaway camp for arts and drama, where I fit in just beautifully, at least at first. The rest of the drama queens had big, bold stories too; finally, we were all playing the same game. These girls knew how to have a tea party, how to sit down in front of some plastic cups and saucers and pretend to pour liquid in them and then pretend to drink it, without someone saying, "There's no tea here, this isn't tea, what kind of tea is this, invisible tea?" Because *that's not fun.* Jesus! Just drink your imaginary tea and eat a fucking cookie.

Alas, the usual dynamics kicked in soon enough, and by week three or four, I had started to fray around the edges. Right around this time, coincidentally, I received news from my mother and stepfather that my stepsister Alexandra had died in a car crash. Alexandra was only two years older then me; she and I were practically twins. She was all I could talk about, obviously. This very terrible thing had just happened to me. I cried a lot, which lost its luster quickly; my bunkmates ignored me, so I cried more. I was the most authentically depressed urchin in our finale performance of "Oliver!" and I left camp bereft not only of my stepsister, but of any ongoing friendships I might have once hoped for with my erstwhile campmates.

So I have decided not to bring Alexandra's death to school with me. And the cancer thing – that's old. I don't talk about that anymore. Not with people at school, anyway. That's what I have my online friends for. They've been through it too, they get it. They know how hard it is, acting like we care about the shallow, meaningless bullshit our peers concern themselves with, when we've seen the curtain between life and death flutter before our eyes, felt the ticking of finite time in our marrow-starved bones.

It's a good thing AOL doesn't charge by the hour anymore; somebody at home might try to stop me from my marathon online sessions. Chip has already added another phone line at home, because people keep complaining that ours is always busy when they call, and he is ready to buy another computer for my room so I can still use it for all the school stuff I'm doing while being out of his home office/his hair.

If only I were not voracious for human contact. If only I weren't so very good at lying to myself, among others, at allowing myself to believe that people like me. Take Paige – I still get the feeling from her, when we hang out alone after math, that she enjoys my company, as long as nobody else is around. And why shouldn't she? I am far more interesting than anybody else we know; I am an excellent listener and sayer of pertinent and helpful things; I will share everything I have and steal anything I don't. Most of all, I am funny.

All the girls think so. Getting me to pay for things is funny for a week or two. Calling me "Betsy-Wetsy," insisting that it's a term of endearment and chiding me for having no sense of humor, is funny. Daring me to do something like mouth off to a teacher, then saying, "I can't believe you did that!" is funny. Getting me to write a book report for Dakota, who has never treated me with anything except contempt, is especially funny – I actually think she's asking because she wants to get to know me better, and that this favor I'm doing her is going to make her like me, finally. And that's hilarious.

One bright spot: the guidance counselor, Ms. Mulhern. I am referred to her by my homeroom/science/history teacher, Mr.

Seims, who finds me as irritating as everyone else does, but either hopes that Ms. Mulhern will be able to help me clean up my act and be less of a pain in the ass, or really dislikes Ms. Mulhern.

The frizzy, idealistic, gooey-centered Ms. Mulhern ("Please, call me Judith") talks a lot, which saves me from saying too much, and our conferences become the highlight of my week. She's one of the first adults who will carry water for me: She makes excuses for my behavior, spins my faults as favorable traits, defends me against valid accusations by others.

"Well, it's no wonder you're acting up in class, Hon, you've done so much bopping around in your life; if you had some stability, maybe you could catch your breath and settle down a little, but what does anybody expect, when you've never stayed put anywhere for more than a few months at a time..."

I am only scheduled to see Ms. Mulhern once per week, but she has granted me an extra session during lunch on Tuesdays. I try to walk by her office first and last thing every day; sometimes she has a minute for me, sometimes she is with someone else. When she is with someone else, I find myself incensed, and I want to bang my fist against the door until both fist and door are broken. She is the only reason I don't refuse to go to school at all.

Towards the end of the year I start being almost-friends with Tim and Danielle, both of whom are into things like prank calls, party lines, and ordering pizzas for people they don't like. They are a strange, non-romantic couple; within ten years, they will both come out as gay. They let me hang around with them, but they have a special twin language they speak that makes them cackle with laughter, and it is clear that I am there to watch only.

When the prank phone calls start coming to my house, honestly, it could be anybody.

Findings: Frog is really hot; frog gets the point. Frog no longer wishes to participate in experiment.

Stage Three: Seventh grade

Oh, god. Let's make this quick. I lie, okay? I lie big. I tell everyone that my latest semi-annual screening came back positive, my cancer has returned, and I get busted by the school nurse, who calls my mother and is informed that no such recurrence has occurred. A communication to this effect is circulated amongst my teachers. The situation becomes public knowledge within a day.

Just imagine your worst humiliation broadcast to the most people possible. Picture people laughing at you to your face, telling you what a psycho you are, how pathetic. Imagine finding no consolation or refuge anywhere. Acquiring endless nicknames. Being the psychic piñata for a group of shrieking, over-privileged twelve and thirteen year olds with asshole parents whose ugliest traits they delightedly mimic while they beat you to death with sticks.

After three days of this, I refuse to go to school. Why? I don't need to finish junior high; my life is over. All I can do is obsess about re-doing that day, the day I decided my cancer came back and everybody should know it. I can so clearly see myself arriving at school without having purposely cried my face swollen, and avoiding Paige entirely, and certainly not saying to her that I am very upset because I have bad news. I imagine how unremarkable the day would have been, with only the usual slights and provocations; I marvel at how awful I thought my life was, before I experienced this.

Couldn't I just turn the dial back? Just one notch? Just…click! And it's back to the way it was? Can't we reset? I can see this alternate reality so perfectly; it's right there. Why can't I access it?

Anna and Chip demand that I return to school, going so far as to take me there personally in a chauffeured town car in the morning and pick me up in the afternoon in the same. I am also sent to see a psychoanalyst, Judy, who I visit three times per week in her Upper West Side apartment/office. I lay down on Judy's couch and say whatever the fuck I want, and she…I don't know. Says, "Mmm," at times, and not at others. Doesn't interrupt, at least; doesn't judge. Talking to Judy is actually pretty calming, when it's not impossibly agitating; I credit Judy – along with self-harm and my rich online life – with making it possible for me to live through these months.

School remains an active, flaming, sulfurous hell tended by

demons with red-hot pitchforks and nothing better to do but poke me with them. I still get to see Ms. Mulhern, but she clearly doesn't love me as much as she once did. She lets me sit in her office once a week, but she doesn't tell me why nothing is my fault anymore. Why not? *It's still not my fault.* I didn't ask for this, just like nobody asks for cancer.

It's time for me to start working on my suicide note.

Result: Frog is dead. You happy now?

6

Wait I'm Confused

There was a new admission on Wednesday. I don't like it one bit. I find it destabilizing. I should have made sure my former roommate Courtney didn't go home; I didn't know how good I had it with ol' Courtney, she who played the violin of her inner arm with a razor bow. I should have sabotaged her and got her to stay.

But the bed was empty, so they put the new girl in my room. Stacy. Her family is Colombian, and she's gorgeous. Petite, voluptuous, smirking; long, thick hair. *Very* upsetting. Put anybody else in my room and put her in theirs, because I can't take her. I'm under enough stress.

I have never smelled toiletries like hers. They must be made of pure pheromones. She smells like mango and mint and cocoa and warmth. Her toes are plump grapes, their crescent nails silver. She has a tattoo on her right ankle, a dusky black cross. You can see the hair follicles on her calves, and I want to BITE HER LEG.

I should clarify: I don't want to have sex with Stacy. I don't want to have sex with anybody, but least of all Stacy. I can imagine nothing more awkward or embarrassing. I have observed that sex alienates people as often as it draws them in, and that is the opposite of my intent. Unfortunately, biting someone's leg above the ankle tattoo is also alienating, which is why we don't bite people anymore.

I don't want to have sex with her. I want to be her best best best best friend. I want to lie next to her in bed and cuddle her and be cuddled by her. I want to play with her hair. I want to talk about the weird dreams we had. I want people to refer to us as "Stacenbetty." I want her to be all mine and nobody else's. I want to hug her and pet her and squeeze her and call her George.

This is the type of shit that got me in here in the first place. This is exactly the kind of situation I've been in here to avoid.

Maureen the counselor loves Stacy. Everybody loves her, even the ones who don't. She doesn't have to be talking to have us all looking at her; she can just sit in group, right leg crossed over left, flip flop gaping seductively away from her size-five sole as her foot dangles. Was somebody else talking? Just Tara: blah blah body image, blah blah bulimia. (Though I will give Tara credit for her commitment: She has burst blood vessels in her eye with her violent puking. She's not skating by on dry heaves, like some of these fakers.)

But even as Maureen has leaned forward towards Tara, knitting her forehead to show exactly how hard she's listening, you can't fail to notice that her own right leg is crossed over her left, mirroring Stacy next to her, towards whom Maureen is unwittingly leaning, ostensibly just tipping her head to one side to facilitate her concentration, but in reality listing like a shipwreck in progress, because that's what happens around Stacy: Everybody's magnetic north flips, their compasses go nuts, and sailors hurl themselves overboard at the sound of the siren.

"Does anybody recognize what Tara's describing?" asks Maureen, and we all look at Stacy.

There is no silent crying, there is no squeezing my fists so hard the fingernails dig painfully into the palms, there is no hyperventilation or trigger reaction or St. Vitus Dance I can perform to swing attention my way. I could raise my hand and tell Maureen that I've suddenly realized she's been right all along: My oppositional defiance is a vestigial coping mechanism that no longer serves me, and I've realized that the value of honest relationships where you risk being vulnerable is greater than the value of this false self I've created as a shield against intimacy, and, as such, I'm ready to shut down the kicking-myself-in-the-ass machine I call a personality and start honoring my truth. She'd nod and turn to her left and say, "Stacy, what do you think about what Betty's saying?"

I can't sleep. I can't sleep in the same room as her. It's not just her; I was spinning before she got here, lying awake, mind racing. It's not Stacy. It's everything. It's Lily. Most of all, it's me.

I don't feel like myself lately. I don't even know what that means.

A year ago, Lily was assigned to me, in much the same way Stacy was last week. By fiat of the Schoenfeld Academy's dorm authority, Lily was selected to be my roommate for our junior year of high school; by fiat of fate, she was selected to be the love of my life.

It hurts to write her name. It hurts to say it, to taste the pungent absence, and it hurts not to say it. I haven't talked about Lily with anybody here; out of all the phantoms who might plague me at night, she is the only one that's gone unnamed. I've been trying my hardest to make her not exist. After all the people in my life I've called into existence, can't I call this one out of it?

I can't, I know. I wouldn't want to, either. But sometimes I feel like her death might be the only thing that could redress the pain of losing her. The fact that she's walking around alive on Earth without me in her life is physically impossible for me to bear, and, short of me finding her and handcuffing myself to her forever, she might honestly have to die or move to New Zealand in order for me to ever have any peace again.

I wonder how "normal" people do it. I wonder how "normal" people deal with their unrequited feelings, or even their requited ones; how they love other people without going crazy from anxiety and jealousy and stress. I've comforted myself all these years by assuming that most "normal" people are lacking, dead inside, with no soul or imagination, and their loves are superficial, atavistic responses to biological and cultural imperatives, instead of the spiritual, alchemical homecoming of the infinite self to its other half that I experienced with Lily. I don't know anymore.

I am like a newly separated conjoined twin, once fused at the cranium to my perfect double, now missing half my head.

It may be too soon for me to talk about it.

———

So let's talk about Anna, the original heartbreak. That's what I'm here to resolve, right? With the psychic support of Dr. Jen, Dinah, the counselors, and my peers, I will finally be able to address the pain I've tried to avoid all these years, and I will be healed. It's time, so they tell me, for me to "trade the hurt of suffering for the hurt of healing," because "healing eventually heals, but suffering stays an open wound forever."

I get it. Handy metaphor. Too bad it doesn't always work that way. Some wounds don't heal. It's like, if a shark bites off your arm, the stump can heal all it wants, and that's great, but your arm isn't going to grow back. It's just not.

My mother is here for our bi-monthly family therapy session. I realize that she hasn't looked me in the eyes since I got back from Florida eight years ago. She'll look at my eyebrows, or my forehead, or my ears; she'll fluff my hair or peck my cheek, but she won't meet my eyes. She's never wanted to hug me; I don't know why, but I'm used to it by now. It would be nice if she could at least stand to look at me.

In therapy she addresses Dr. Jen. I'm sitting right next to her, but she says to Dr. Jen, "Beth...*Betty* is so angry at me."

I don't know why she even bothers coming every week. It's not for my sake. She doesn't give a shit about me. She only comes because she knows how bad it would look if she didn't show up. She knows they'd close my file, stamp "FUCKED UP BY BITCH MOM" on the front, and everyone would call it a day and go get some beers and maybe do some karaoke. She's got to come and play the victim to make sure everybody remembers who the problem is.

Aww, poor Anna – she's hurt that I'm angry at her! I love when people get hurt because you're angry at them. Doesn't she get it? I never wanted to be angry in the first place! I'm only angry at her because *she* hurt *me!* *I'm* the one who's hurt! She doesn't get to be hurt! She hurt me, which made me be angry at her, and now she's the one who's hurt? Bullshit! And no, I won't stop yelling!

Also, "Beth...*Betty*." Come on. It's been years since we made that change. She does it to be provocative. I don't refer to her as "*Eanna*bel." I'm not going to rise to the bait.

Dr. Jen nods. She says, "I know we've discussed some of the reasons she's felt that way. Do you feel like you can accept Betty feeling angry at you?"

Speaking of provocative, why are we talking about what my mother can and can't accept? This is supposed to be about *me*. It's not like I'm not trying here, people; I do want to learn something, if I can. Psychology and human behavior are among my most active fields of interest.

I have to breathe deeply – not so I can faint, but so I can keep myself from screaming. Anna wants me to scream. If I scream, I look crazy. If I look crazy, she wins.

"Well, I don't really have a choice," says my mother – my pitiable, put-upon mother, with her platinum credit card and her sham "home fashion consulting" business; with the husband who dotes on her and the condo in St. Thomas they bought while I was in exile down in Florida, eight years old and fending off my senile grandfather in his thin pajamas in the middle of the night. "I have to accept it."

Dr. Jen parries. "You have to accept it, but *can* you? *Will* you? I think Betty needs to know that you're okay with her anger. Not that you like it – you don't have to like it. But that you're okay with it, and you're not going to love her less for it."

"Of course," says Anna, meaning that she'll accept my anger, that she won't love me less. "Of course."

It's easy for her to say this. She could not love me any less than she does.

Satisfied by this big score, that my criminally neglectful mother will allow me to be angry at her from within the confines of a psychiatric clinic for an hour twice per month, Dr. Jen turns to me. "Betty? What's going on with you right now?"

Me? I'm just sitting here in my chair, clenching my kegel

muscles like I do every second of my life, because I've been touched too many times in the wrong places by the wrong people, and I will never feel safe again. Just feeling the blood stomping through my temporal arteries, kicking me in the head. What the fuck does it matter? Nothing matters. Nothing my mother says is going to change how I feel. Even if she owned up to all of it – well, that would be nice, but it still wouldn't matter. Whatever it is that's wrong with me isn't going away.

"Nothing," I say, glum.

I get the Dr. Jen cocked eyebrow. "Betty?"

I give the Patient Betty folded arm-cross. "I've said everything already."

Her, bemusedly: "It doesn't appear as though you feel like you've been heard."

Me, truculent: "She knows."

I know we're all play-acting here, but give me a break, old lady. Don't make me say it again. It doesn't change. Leave my shark stump alone.

You want to know what never grows back? A father. My mother never gave me the chance to have one; to this day, she refuses to tell me his name. She's done a lot of damage in my life, but denying me a father of any sort – in our private sessions, Dinah agrees that it's done me *irreparable* psychic harm.

I want a father. He doesn't have to be a good one; he doesn't have to be in my life at all. He can even be dead. I could accept that. All I want is someone I can look at in a picture and say, *That, for sure, is the man who is my father. I am not made entirely from my mother. Here is another piece of me.*

I used to use my missing father as a ploy for pity, before I understood how commonplace it is. I don't expect pity for it anymore – I have to reach much farther these days to extrude sympathy from people, even from myself; in the meantime, I lacerate myself for whining about something so banal and trivial. It's not like I'm a refugee of genocide, or a victim of political torture. I'm aware how much worse most people in the world have it than me. My problems aren't bad enough for how bad I feel, and that makes me feel like shit.

"Grandpa," I say quietly, and I start to cry.

My seventh grade suicide note read, in part, "I hope everybody who was mean to me is happy now that I'm dead like they wanted."

It was tempting to get more specific than that, to name names and detail offenses, but it would have turned into a six or seven page affair, easy, and I felt like that would dilute its impact. Now that I think about it, what I should have done was write separate notes to specific people – well, it's not too late.

It was a decent first-draft suicide note. Very formal language, a testament to my seriousness, with no contractions ("I have not known...I do not wish...I cannot live..."), nor colloquialisms, nor humor. I read it through several times, trying to see it through the eyes of someone different each time – Anna, Ms. Mulhern, Erin, Heather Glazer. My internet friends. Strangers. So tragic, such an intelligent girl, such a talented writer; so sensitive, so cruelly rebuffed, so vastly misunderstood. It was heartrending, right? But was it heartrending *enough*?

I only got as far as the note that time. That was enough. I kept the note in the drawer of my desk where I kept important things, like the plastic wings they gave me on my first solo flight to Florida, and my letters from Laurent from cancer camp. I felt prepared. In the days and weeks after writing the note, anytime I felt untenably awful (i.e., all the time), I'd think, *Well, all I have to do is go home, pull out the note, and take a bunch of pills.* Then I'd daydream about how fucked up everybody would be by my death until I felt better.

But instead of killing myself quickly and permanently, I decided to become bulimic. I had to do *something* that would get me out of school, preferably something that would land me in the hospital, and there was no sexier disease to have in the eighth grade than bulimia. As reviled as I was, if I was bulimic, people would want to hang out with me just in case I was contagious.

Here again: an example of honest work. There are no shortcuts to bulimia. You can pretend to throw up behind a bathroom door, tossing sink water into the toilet to make that audible splash, but that only goes so far. Sooner or later, you're going to need the bilious breath, the traces of yellowish crust, and for that, you need the real thing. It's harder than most people want to give you credit for.

You need to be strong to overcome the body's instincts. The body doesn't want to throw up. The body wants you to take the toothbrush out of its throat, away from the gag reflex; it would also like you, while you're at it, to take a look at yourself in the mirror and ask yourself, *What the hell am I doing?* The body would like to remind you that you're both on the same side here, you're supposed to be working together, and what has it ever done to you to deserve what you're doing to it?

When the body finally gives in, it's not going quietly. It's going to hurt. Your whole torso will feel like it's herniating, like you're being squeezed around the ribs by a mustachioed strongman in a wrestling singlet. You'll feel the lethargy of dehydration, the arrhythmia straining your heart. Your throat will be raw from acid. When you swallow, it will feel like you're strangling.

This is why I have to respect Tara – I did my time with my head in the toilet. And I know that everybody thinks bulimia is a pussy disorder, the go-to attention-getter for rich girls with daddy issues, but damn. Do it right, and it's hardcore.

Hardcore as it may have been, my bulimia crisis did not land me in inpatient care. This was surprising; I would have sworn that Anna was ready to send me away again. I'd been keeping my head down at home, trying not to be a nuisance, spending most of my time online, but even with my head down, I was a disaster. I needed to be escorted to and picked up from school, where I necessitated special conferences and meetings; I needed thrice weekly therapy sessions at $250 a pop. Wouldn't it have served everyone's ends if I'd gone away for a little while?

Instead, Chip's insurance paid for an outpatient program at Lenox Hill Hospital, where I joined my very first therapeutic circle of jerks, and was outfitted with medication to address my various issues: Zoloft for depression, Xanax for anxiety. A veritable Scrabble board of useless letters. The Xanax was pleasant, but it made me feel stupid; the Zoloft didn't change my mood any, but at least it killed my appetite – way better than puking.

Three months of bulimia, believe it or not, was the thing that finally made people shut their mouths about me at school. At first, it was something else to mock, but soon everybody could see me suffering, my haggard look and baggy clothes weren't faked, and if anybody dared look at me, I threw them a look larded with accusation – *Look, I'm killing myself. Isn't this what you wanted? Are you happy now?*

In those days, it was still culturally acceptable to make fun of the kids who were "on the spectrum" (though we had very few true infrareds at our school), and you were allowed to slut-shame Evelyn Drechsler for having given blow jobs to some freshmen guys from Trinity. You could even make fun of the way the deaf guy at the corner deli spoke – it's not like he was going to hear you. But publicly making fun of an eating disorder was somehow off-limits.

Had I known this in advance, I would have skipped the cancer and gone straight to bulimia.

Stacy knows what she's doing. You don't smolder like that accidentally. Her breath is just barely audible all day long; it's like the sound of the ocean when you're near her, a soothing white noise that resets your own breath to its tempo. Her chest swells – and believe me, it's plenty swell to begin with – then subsides, swells then subsides, *ssshhh*, like the tide. She puts her fingers in her hair and pulls it back, twists it into an unbound ponytail, and apposite wisps jump out to frame her lovely face.

She comes over to me as I'm standing next to my dresser. I hold my breath so the smell of her lotion doesn't overwhelm my limbic system. She picks up my hand and kind of joggles it, weighing it in hers.

"Beh-heh-heh-hetty," she says, *adorably*. "It's so boring here."

Get thee behind me, Stacy.

I have no doubt that she's bored. It is insufferably boring here. That's a big part of the point of treatment, to bore you into cracking and then bore you back together. But I am interesting to Stacy, though it's more for what I know than for who I am – she knows if there's anything fun or worthwhile to do here, I've found it. Whatever powerful attraction I also happen to exude is *pro forma* to her, I'm sure: useful, but not all that noteworthy.

I am not bored with Stacy around. She is all that is happening here. She is what's for dinner. She is the movie of the week. You can't not watch her. When her mother shows up for family counseling, she's like a celebrity; we're all casually walking past the waiting area, trying to check her out, this tiny, stout, be-furred woman with the glamour-puss face and the dime-sized emerald earrings who somehow produced this fascinating person.

"I want to dooooooo something."

I don't waste time being envious of girls like Stacy anymore. I'm not going to compete with her for the kind of attention she attracts; that'd be like her competing with me in math. Why sign up for a fight where you know you're getting clobbered?

No, my maxim is, "If you can't beat them, assimilate them." I.e., the next best thing to being Stacy is being next to Stacy. If I were going to be envious of anybody, I'd be envious of Stacy's roommate, or whomever she chose to spend the most time with; since that person has proved to be me, I have no object for my free-floating envy, and it just wafts around burning my sinuses like a bug bomb.

Hence, perhaps, my clouded judgment. "What do you want to dooooooo?" I ask.

"I don't knooooooooow," she says. She is still holding my hand, swinging it like a second-grader. "Something fun."

Bee boo boo boop beep... My internal computer gets right to work; speaks to me in its most alluring female robot voice. Fun: That which you are not supposed to do. Getting away with things. See: stealing, pranking, breaking rules, leaving the facility.

"You want to fuck with somebody?" I suggest.

Stacy jerks downward on my arm. "Yes!" She is delighted by my perspicacity. That is exactly what she wants, but could not have given words to, or even a reason for – if you were to ask her why she wants to fuck with somebody, she'd have no real idea.

All she knows is that she *wants*. She doesn't know what, why, or how.

I get that.

We decide to fuck with Ophira. It's unfair – Ophira is way too easy – but we're not out to hurt her. We just want to pull her string and watch her jump. She's like a jack-in-the-box; you turn her crank, and she'll pop out screaming, "MY SLIPPERS ARE GONE! WHO TOOK MY SLIPPERS! I SWEAR TO GOD, MY *GRANDMOTHER* GAVE ME THOSE SLIPPERS, THEY'RE *VINTAGE*, AND IF I DON'T GET THEM BACK BACK IN *TWO SECONDS* I AM GOING TO *CALL THE POLICE AND PRESS CHARGES FOR THEFT* – DON'T TELL ME TO CALM DOWN!"

We're not actually going to keep the slippers. That would be mean. We're simply going to withhold them for a few minutes, then put them in the lounge, under whichever chair she was last seen occupying. That way, when her slippers are found almost immediately in a likely place, and she starts screaming, "BUT I DIDN'T LEAVE THEM IN THE LOUNGE! THEY WERE UNDER MY BED!", the counselors will think it's just Ophira being Ophira, always blaming other people for her carelessness instead of taking responsibility, and the angrier she gets at their refusal to believe her, the funnier it will be.

Stacy's face is flushed as we skulk towards the room Ophira shares with Abby (Histrionic, 301.50 – absent father, no boundaries, huge-time slut). We only have a few minutes before lunch, and we need this to go down before we all leave the dorm area for the meal and then afternoon therapy, because we have to make sure we're here to witness it when she goes monkeyshit.

I feel extremely happy and reckless and strong. I feel Stacy cleaving to me because I have produced a new kind of good feeling in her right now. It's not the everyday, ho-hum good-enough feeling she's learned to squish out of being admired and desired all the time; she's got a high tolerance for that. She can make that for herself. This is something she needs me for, this thought-state we create between us, the tingling electrochemical mist whose effect I can only describe as "fizzy lifting drink."

Stacy leads, passing Ophira and Abby's open door; seeing only Abby inside, she signals for me to hang back. I watch from the hall as she stops in the doorway, droops languidly, and complains, "Abba-babba-babby, I'm so bored."

Three minutes and one purloined slipper later (we could only get one – better than none – maybe even better than two, actually), as we're shuffling to the lounge for the drop, Stacy slides her arm tight under mine and takes my hand again, pulling us right alongside each other, our conjoined knuckles managing to skim both her breast and mine. I draw back reflexively, and she feels the startle she gave me. I feel her smiling at my side.

I don't think I give Stacy enough credit. She knows exactly who she wants to fuck with, why, and how.

Okay, fine: Lily.

Nope. The internet. Let's talk about the internet instead.

My first screen names included: timebombbb, themissinggirl, mskittyscratch, evrybdyhtsme, TheRobbie, TylerMcKenzie, ninjabloodbeth, zerOhOpez, JustAnotherSurvivor, Prozaic, CathyStageTwo, lovednlost, scarredgrrl, cuttinglinguist, Frances_Been, CindyForever, msmentalhell, skeletonskale, never2thin, and, when necessary, AnnaMadigan.

Oh, the golden age of anonymity on the internet! Things used to be so much easier, before all this irksome "transparency." I'm surprised I ever came up for air at all during junior high. Even today, having of necessity scaled back by at least four-fifths on my activity, it's so time- and energy-consuming – I sometimes wonder if my "return on investment, these days," as Chip would say, is "a break-even."

But back then...oh, back then...

Flashback: A young girl sits at the desk in her room behind a computer monitor large and boxy enough to obscure her from the casual glance of any would-be observers. No one can see her face in the cathode glow, her premature squint as she flips through the tiled browser windows, each one a wormhole into another reality: she needs an organ transplant, she is training to be an Olympic figure skater, she is worried about the man who hurt her being released from jail. She is a level ten mage, a sexy stewardess, a vampire. She is trying to escape from a cult. She is whatever she says she is, for as long as she says so. She is pulsing with the possibilities of her life.

She is called to the table by her mother, who also has a fake name, but refuses to see how that might parallel her daughter's situation in any way. The food has been prepared by a woman named Verna, a personal chef from across the park. Anna speaks to Verna by phone every morning and receives the delivery of her meals every afternoon, unless she's out; then the doorman takes them for her until she can get back from the *nothing* she does all day.

The girl helps her mother unpack the containers from the bag, puts forks and knives and napkins on the table. Her mother says "thanks" in the tossed-off way you say it to someone who props the door open for a second as they exit ahead of you.

"Sure," says the girl helpfully, because she longs to feel helpful, maybe even needed, and her haste to drop what she was doing to help unpack and set, while Chip lingers on his own computer until the food has hit the bowls before he saunters in to feed, is meant to show the sincerity of this wish. To impress favorably upon her mother. To be good. She would like to be good. She really would.

But she's not even there. She's physically present at the table, but as with a lucid dream, she is aware that this isn't really "real." She knows that all of her life is in her head: There is no sound without her eardrums to strain it; there is no tangible "blue" in the blue sky she sees, only a conspiracy of atoms to produce that idea in her mind. Everything her mind does constantly – all the remembering, forecasting, observing as though from without – this is what she was born with. Everything inside her is what is real. All the rest of the shit going on around her – that's nothing.

Chip is nothing. Whenever Chip opens his mouth, she hears a noise like a vacuum cleaner at full blast – BWAAAAAAAANNH BWAAAAANNH BWAAAAAAANNH. She can't hear anything he's saying. Ordinarily, he sounds unctuous, like a TV newsman;

she knows that from talking to him in the past. For the past six months it's just been BWWAAAAAAAAAAANH.

He's a fraud, and her mother knows it. That hearty, faux-relaxed, bad-actor manner of his; the *over-inflection*... and the in*tent*ional *pau*ses...in his speech... – that's so people don't worry about where their principal of their money is, beyond the breezy assurance that it's "parked in the Virgin Islands, where Uncle Sam can't touch it" (psst, *because it doesn't exist anymore*).

That's why there's always so much stuff on the dining table: dusty, unlit candles in sticks, a vase with flowers, a pitcher of water and a bottle of wine, seventeen bottles of vitamins and supplements. Catalogs. That way they don't have to see each other as they eat. They can make small talk while looking at other things. "You want some of this?" Chip says, looking at the salad he's extending towards the girl instead of looking at her.

And yet you can see, in the way Anna nervously trails her hand over Chip's back as she passes his chair to get to the kitchen, there's genuine tenderness between them. Because he is a fraud, and so is she, and they both know it. They're like protected witnesses: They are the only ones who know each other's true identity. The desperate gratitude you feel for the one person you don't have to lie to in life – that's love.

Maybe if I knew her less well, she could feel that kind of comfort with me. But I am both too much of a mirror to her, and not enough of one.

I don't think she looks in her own eyes very often either.

When the young girl is excused, after she takes her plate and cutlery into the kitchen, rinses them in the sink, and places them in the dishwasher, she goes back to her room to resume the work of being all these people. She has a lot of email and IMs to answer.

Jenny, one of her cancer friends, wants to know how the consult with the surgeon went the other day. Jenny's email is festooned with a string of alternating tildes and asterisks, meant to represent the good health and healing "vibes" she sends the girl's way; the quotes in her email signature include, "Cancer is a word, not a sentence," (unattributed) and, "Never, never, never give up" (Winston Churchill, referring to the bombing of London).

The girl replies: Not so good, sorry I didn't write yesterday, feeling very down. How are you today? Hope you're feeling better. Sorry I don't have more to say, just feeling hopeless today. Tilde, asterisk, tilde.

To her vampire friends: Tried to stay indoors today but had to leave the house in daylight, now I feel like I have a sunburn on my soul.

To Amanda, from her thinspo group: Sorry I didn't write back sooner. Everything feels hopeless today. No matter how thin I get, I will never love myself, because I am a piece of crap. Everybody who knows me hates me. See, this is why I didn't want to write, because it's all stupid crap, but I didn't want you to think I was ignoring you, because when I thought you were ignoring me I was suicidal (j/k). Sorry. Sorry for being me.

To the cutters: I don't want to trigger anyone but I am having a BAD night and I can't stop thinking about how good it would feel not to feel this way...

To the cutters, minutes later: I know I shouldn't think like that. I'm sorry. I want to be positive and strong but I'm not. I wish I could do or say ANYTHING that wasn't the exact wrong thing.

To Royce, the forty-year-old guy from San Francisco, via IM: We heard about dick cheese in health class. It sounds disgusting. Yeah. They made the boys and girls go into different rooms to talk about their bodies. Wait – ugh, my stepfather wants another drink or something. C u soon.

She's worked assiduously for months to create and sustain all these relationships. If she were to show up online without finding a flurry of new messages and emails, she would feel humiliated. (Humiliated? In front of who? In front of herself, with her stupid hopes all over her ugly face like an idiot, and then they're dashed because you suck and that's what you deserve, and you know damn well nobody cares about you unless you trick them into it, HA HA, I can't believe you can still kid yourself into thinking anybody's going to care about you; out of all the lying you do, it's the lying to yourself that's the most pathetic.) She'd be wracked with resentment and revenge fantasies – *If I'm so important to everybody, where the hell are they? I'm dying! I'm suicidal! I'm starving to death! And nobody cares whether I live or die. Fine, I'll just be dead, then, if that's what they want.*

Then sometimes she experiences all her correspondence as a burden. Sometimes the resentment is there, no matter how many chimes and pings and you've-got-mail's she hears. Everybody always wanting things from her. The lengths she has to go to in order to keep anybody in her life. It's unfair. Why can't she be cared about just for being her, the way everyone else gets to be? She wants to drop the whole thing sometimes: the whole phone book of names and numbers, the entire dictionary of damage done. It's so much weight to carry.

Meanwhile, in Anna and Chip's room, more lies being told over email and IM: We'd love to attend the benefit, but our daughter has a recital that night. I'm so sorry we weren't there – our daughter had a high fever and we didn't feel right leaving her alone. Are you sure they didn't receive the check? Well, give it another day, and if it hasn't come by tomorrow, I'll stop payment and issue a new one.

The girl opens her closet door, half-hidden as she fishes around in the corner. Why is she worried? Nobody's going to interrupt her. Nobody's going to check on her, if that's what she thinks. There's a special shoebox with a snapshot of a pair of sandals on the front; inside is a bottle of cough syrup, some sunburn cream, some antibiotic ointment, some paper towels from the girls' room at school, and an Exact-o knife. She stops moving and listens. Nobody is coming, nobody is ever coming. She begins.

She unscrews the top from the cough syrup and takes a belt. She didn't eat a lot of dinner, because the less she eats the worse her mother feels, so it hits her *nice* and fast. She replaces the cough syrup, gets out the sunburn cream. She slides it across the skin of her left shoulder, where a small thicket of thorny, red sticks is collecting, one slash at a time. It's not as numbing as she'd like, but it's better than nothing.

The sunburn cream goes away. The Exact-o knife and the antibiotic ointment come out. I take a deep breath and do what needs to be done, and then it's over. It stings. I don't really enjoy it. Other people report a sense of calm, a desire to see the blood flow. I have neither. I have a sense of accomplishment. I blot the wound and swipe it with ointment. The kit is returned to its home in the corner.

This is a true story, or so I told myself at the time. I was having some trouble differentiating between what was made up, and what felt true, and what had become true in the retelling. But any time I got too far from the truth, I could consider the physical proof, the tangible expression of my torment:

The cuts on my upper arms. The medications in my bathroom. The treatment bills that came in. The barf that came out.

That's how I knew it was real.

7

Her Loss

I dreamt of Lily last night.

I've had this nightmare for years. Some woman that I desperately need is taunting and rejecting me, I feel myself becoming physically violent, and I warn myself as I lunge at her, *Don't do this; this never, ever works out well,* but it's too late – I've already bit off a chunk of her face, or her scalp, and a crowd is collecting around us, all pointing and yelling at me, and I want to kill myself because I did it *again.* I ruined everything beyond repair.

So last night it's Lily's long black hair in my teeth as I bite her on the back of her neck, right where her skull meets her spine. It's Lily shrieking at me to stop, go away, leave her alone for the rest of her life. And – God, just describing this is making me want to stab myself in the leg with a knife – I'm begging, pleading, *I'm sorry, I didn't mean to, please don't hate me, I don't want it to be like this!*

Which is not exactly how it happened in real life. But close enough.

She was assigned to me. Did I say that? I'm starting to get fuzzy on what we've covered here. Well, it's important enough to say twice. Ours was an arranged match; when we started living together, we were strangers. The only thing we knew about each other was, "This is a person with whom I will share a home."

I guess I'm harping on it because I want to make it clear: I didn't choose her. She showed up in my life. And I don't believe in attributing things to "fate," or "everything happens for a reason," or "when God opens the window he shuts the blinds and closes an umbrella," or whatever he supposedly does. But I do believe – very fervently believe, whether I always act on it or not – in embracing what is.

And this was the missing piece of my soul. This stringy girl who came through the door with six family members and two duffel bags, with her big dumb felt hat and her fractal posters and her crystal deodorant stone – she was the answer to the riddle I didn't know I'd been asked.

This isn't some kind of roommate fetish, by the way. I don't automatically go berserk for every girl I share a room with (see: Courtney the cutter). I would have had the same reaction to Stacy regardless of whose room she shared; same with Lily. Other than that, the situations have nothing in common.

Lily isn't a knockout like Stacy is. You can catch your breath around Lily, you can even breathe easy. She's lovely, of course – she has a kind of drowning naiad beauty, with her long face and drooped eyes, unglamorous and ungroomed. Thinking about Lily's face makes me wish I were any good at drawing. I would much rather look at Lily's face than try to shield my eyes from Stacy's.

I know what a sap I sound like, rhapsodizing over a perfectly ordinary seventeen-year-old girl simply because she was the one who stepped over my threshold that day. And I am a sap, also a simp, a sucker, and a chump. I keep having to remind myself that *Lily is nothing special.* She is a wealthy white girl from the suburbs of Connecticut, she is interchangeable with every Ashley and Brittany and Carly out there, and her eco-hippie Wiccan aesthetic does not substantively distinguish her from anybody else, no matter how many braided hemp bracelets she bears.

And now we're back to what I love about her. She is so *her.* She is 100 percent committed to the whole Lily act. Her consistency is comforting, such a contrast from my labile moods. I could always walk through a store, or down a sidewalk, and hone right in on the clothes Lily would choose; I could always see her thinking, with every decision she faced: How many owls will be affected negatively by this action?

Some context would probably help here.

The Schoenfeld Academy is a well-known boarding school in the Northeast, catering primarily to the kind of rich-kid fuck-up who isn't so fucked up that they need to be sent to Costa Rica or one of those horse farm schools. Its academics program is strong; its students are not. It doesn't matter. They'll go to college or they won't; they'll go windsurfing for a year or two, try to do some acting, and then live off their parents until it's time for rehab. So it's more of a daycare center than an actual place of learning.

I wound up there after a tumultuous eighth, ninth, and tenth grades spent elsewhere —several elsewheres, which I may detail later, if it becomes pertinent – after which, Anna and Chip presented me with several brochures and a lecture. As always, it was presented as my best interests being served.

My mother sat next to Chip on the sofa, her hands clasped in her lap as she emphasized her concern for me.

"Honey, we love you, and we want you to get the help and support and structure you need."

I sat across from them on the chair, trying to decode this unfamiliar sentence. Who was "Honey"? When had Anna ever called me that? And "we love you"... what was that supposed to mean? That's not something we said in our household. I'd been waiting forever for my mother to say she loved me, but instead she said "*we* love you," which was patently untrue.

For a second, I let myself think she was sincere, that she wrung her hands for me and not for herself. That I was Honey, that I'd always been her Honey; that she loved me and wanted to help me.

Then she pushed the pamphlets for various boarding schools my way, and I understood: She loved and wanted to help me so much, she was sending me away. Again.

How stupid of me to think she might actually love me. How stupid of me for wishing she would. I made sure to repeat the word *stupid* about eight thousand times while punching myself in the leg later that night.

Meanwhile, what did Lily do to get sent away? She asked.

Lily comes from this insane blended family: On one side there's her mother, her stepfather, their two kids, and his kid from a previous marriage; then on the other side there's her father, her stepmother, their kid, his kid from the marriage between Lily's mother and current stepmother, *and* the stepmother's two kids from a previous marriage. Lily likes to say, when people ask if she has any brothers and sisters, "Either none, four, or seven, depending on how you want to see it."

Lily's the eldest of all of them by a few years; her youngest sibling was two-year-old Patty, her mother and stepfather's second daughter. With all the family's comings and goings, she was getting "lost in the shuffle" at home – another parent-ism, that passive, evasive phrase. Sure, blame it on the kid, *she* got lost. Blame it on the shuffle. The fact is, *You lost sight of your child.* Lily was *getting lost by her parents.*

She displayed many of the symptoms of lost children: experimentation with alcohol, drugs, sex, white witchcraft, and clove cigarettes. Undue amounts of eyeliner (for a while, in her Goth-ish phase); inept attempts at truancy. These went mostly unnoticed. She had coerced sex and hated herself afterwards; even consensual sex, by the time other people heard and started talking about it, felt ugly and regrettable. But nobody was stopping her from any of it.

Self-harm was not for Lily; she had younger siblings whose welfare she needed to consider. And truth be told, she wasn't all that miserable. She may have been miserable that she wasn't more miserable, if that makes any sense. She suffered from a bit of the *noblesse oblige* – as an able-bodied, neurotypical, straight, white, cisgendered rich girl, she felt that the problems of the world were waiting for her to solve them, and the guilt that she could not do so made her feel acutely plagued by the plight of the impoverished and downtrodden, to whom she compared herself mercilessly all day long.

Point being, she was the one who blew the whistle and said, "I feel like I need to go somewhere I won't be able to get myself into trouble." Isn't that mature? That's the older sister thing, I think; she was like a seventeen-year-old with seven children. She loved her siblings selflessly, the way parents are supposed to but don't, and they selflessly loved her in return.

It was probably this mutual love that gave her such equanimity. To know for certain that you are a loving and loved person – to know that true love comes from within you unbidden, endemically, and to know that this love naturally attracts its return – I can't imagine the feeling of security you would get from knowing that you're essentially a good person. And I have a *really* good imagination.

So there we are, both entering a new high school in our junior year, which we'd both feared would make us oddballs, not realizing that everybody at Schoenfeld Academy is constantly dropping in and out, coming from other rich-kid fuck-up schools, changing custody, being sent to Costa Rica. Me and my new roommate Lily, we're clinging together like stuffed monkeys the first few days, thinking we're the only two of us the world has ever seen; even after this is disproved, we still feel this way.

Our room is on a floor with nineteen others like it – utilitarian, low-ceilinged, the same invariable detritus: stuffed animals on the beds, incense holders on the dressers, Mac laptops, half-empty water glasses, and other students in their all-weather knit hats slumped around the perimeter.

Lily and I have neighbors we like (Dana and Lana: cool, relaxed, makers of puns and dorky references) and neighbors we don't (Rachel and Sierra: bitchy, materialistic, awful taste in music). Lily and I share so many opinions on so many things, and not just because I am agreeing with everything she says, but because when she says them they become indisputably true. And because she gives voice to a lot of the things I think about, things other people never want to address:

"There's so much more to life than we can, like, perceive. We can't even perceive how much there is. And, like, everything is just on this...shallow level..."

Lily has taken psychedelic drugs, about which she is a bit of a zealot; she credits them with awakening her dormant spiritual consciousness. They made her realize, among other things, that "the self is a construct."

I, too, having come to this realization, am interested in her thoughts on it. "When you say 'a construct,' what do you mean?

Like, who does the 'constructing?' What are the, like, 'construction materials?'"

And she's happy I asked. Because over the first week of school, we've sat in on a number of philosophers-stoned conversations that began promisingly enough – "Like, 'the self' is a construct..." – but devolved right away into a mumble of *totally*s and *yaaaaah*s. And asking someone, "What do you mean by that?" is seen not as intellectual curiosity and a desire to better understand them, but as tantamount to glove-slapping them and asking them to name the dueling hour. So interesting things are mentioned, but nothing of interest gets discussed, and the insight about self-construction is revealed as just another piece of self-particleboard.

Not with Lily. She could discuss this shit for hours. "Well, it's like, you're choosing from a...a menu, you know? Like, an infinite menu of things you see around you." She starts pretending to grab things around her, flailing with her octopus arms and gathering empty space.

I am sick right now, writing this, thinking about her octopus arms. I'm wincing away tears. She is so dear and loveable to me; it's so strong I can't bear it. It's like those super sour candies she would sometimes buy, and I'd make her laugh by putting one in my mouth and making horrified faces until I had to drool it out into my hand, yelling, "Candy's not supposed to be painful!"

I don't know whether to skip over the good times or the bad ones. I don't know which ones hurt worse.

———

It was Halloween when Lily first "hooked up with" Michael. You might have thought she'd be averse to that kind of thing, based on the unhappy experiences she'd already endured, but Michael, you see, was different.

Michael was no threat to me. Nobody at school was a threat to me. Most of her back-home friends had receded into lives that didn't overlap with hers – they still had their emails and phone calls and private jokes, but the greatest bond between them had been proximity, not sympathy of worldview. Lily confessed that she found them all a little tedious these days, even her closest back-home friends, Jonah and Heather, whose very existence remained an insult to my peace of mind.

The only people she loved more than me were her siblings, and I hated them for it. It was unfair that they knew her first, they shared the bond of family, and they were guaranteed a seat every year at the Thanksgiving table of her life, while I had to work to earn her love anew every day. I was jealous that they had four parents between them, while I only had half of one. I was also jealous of Lily's parents, who Lily could not help but love and would always need. So even before we got to friends and classmates and dormmates and hookups, I was already walking around in a seething rage over the injustice of the lowly rank I held in her life. But I was like the proverbial kid in the mailroom: I was determined to work my way into the top office, and nobody was going to stop me.

At first, I thought Michael was gay. I'm sure he thought I was gay at first too, so we were both wrong, but I was wronger. By the time I realized that he wanted to have sex with my Lily, he'd already cozied right up to her – *right* up to her; like, I turned around and he was nuzzling her neck. And there is no way that anybody who was "chilling" in our room that night could have missed the expression on my face. I looked like a prisoner who'd just been shanked.

Look, I know some things about the world. I know most people want to have sex with other people, and God knows I'm not about to do any of that with anybody, so, of necessity, they will have to do it with someone else. As such, I suppose I should prefer that Lily be with a milquetoast like Michael, rather than some horrid jock or bro or whatever else they have out there. But I also recognize the danger of the soft person who melts all over you like caramel. A horrid jock might have blown her off; he might have been the one who tipped the scales and made her say, *Enough, I'm not into guys anymore, let's just marry each other and have a bunch of cats and birds and shit.*

Whereas Michael – lethargic, narrow-shouldered, girl-faced Miiiiiiichael (that's how he says his own name, like he's complaining) – he loooooooved her. Still does, no doubt, that imbecile. That goon.

"I know people think I'm gay," I said to Lily one night, week three, after lip-reading what looked like *is she gay or what* from my neighbor Sierra to her friend Adrian while looking directly at me in World Religions that afternoon.

"Booboo!" Lily flapped her octopus arm from her bed and caught me by the forearm, made me sit down next to her. "Whatever you are," she said earnestly, "You're you, and I love you."

One: She called me Booboo. Two: She said I love you. Three: She totally thought I was gay.

Which was fine. The relief of discovering that I wasn't trying to have sex with her, combined with the embarrassment of the mistake and the blow to her ego, would soften her up and leave her that much more open to ingratiation.

"I love you too, Looloo," I said. "But I'm not gay."

Ah, the blushing and the backpedaling and the stammering that ensued – so fetching. Like a shepherdess in an old poem, rosy-cheeked and darling in her discomfiture.

"No, no, it's okay," I assured her, my wry smile saying, *I'm used to it.* "I don't usually talk about it. I let people think whatever they want, you know? I'm good with being seen as whatever."

"Yeah, just because you don't advertise your sexuality all the time doesn't mean you don't have your own thing...." Lily was already jumping to my defense against any straw men who might accuse me of being sexless or a prude.

I interrupted her. "Well, wait...I'm not straight, either." I paused to judge the effect of this on her. She looked confused but determined to remain encouraging. "And...I'm not bi. I'm like...the opposite of bi. Honestly? I think I'm nothing."

"Really? Wow, that's...(briefest possible pause while she tried to figure out exactly what 'that' was)...amazing."

She broke into a huge smile, shook my upper arm, hugged me like I'd just gotten my period for the first time. Like, *Congratulations! Yay! You're asexual!*

"Yeah." I shrugged. "That's why I don't really say anything..."

"No, that's so cool, that's *very* cool." She was legitimately excited about this. Something about the idea of my asexuality was very appealing to her. Maybe it was the idea that she might have a choice in whether or not she ever had sex again, a notion she had obviously never considered before.

I smiled sadly. "I wish it was."

That's the night I told Lily what happened to me.

I started by telling her about the naked game I played with other girls as a child; she laughed and reported a similar instance or two. "It wasn't about having sex with each other," I explained. "It was more about doing something we weren't supposed to do." She nodded and agreed. She hadn't thought about that in years, but it obviously made her happy to remember.

Then I told her about Lillian's brother and the garage, and her face sagged like melting wax. She averted her eyes and bit her lip and held onto my upper arm as I described it.

Lily wanted to know what suffering felt like. She worried all the time that she had not suffered enough, and that some overdue suffering for which she was utterly unprepared was coming for her, big-time; she knew she needed some emotional practice runs. She needed some vicarious suffering. She needed to know what it felt like to be digitally penetrated against your will as you cried and cried, so she could tell whether or not she could take it if it was her, and so she could then decide, yes, it would be awful, but she would live.

I took her there. She held my hand, trembling through it, but working her hardest to show me that there was nothing about this she couldn't handle, nothing that would repulse her or make her feel differently towards me, because (I could hear her thinking) it was *so* important that I knew it wasn't my fault, that it didn't make me dirty or less loveable or bad. Palpable waves of compassion; the sweet smell of her sweat. Every time I paused, she squeezed my hand or shook her head and said, "I'm so, so sorry. I'm so sorry he did that to you."

"I'm sorry to burden you with it," I said, squeezing back. Holding onto her for strength. Forcing a heartbreaking smile through my tortured face.

No, she insisted. It wasn't a burden. She wanted me to be able to talk to her about this, she felt honored that I would be this honest with her, and she wanted me to know that, though it had only been three weeks, she was so incredibly glad she was my roommate, she loved me, she meant it, and not in a superficial social love-ya way. She hugged me, awkwardly rocked me back and forth a few times, looked me full in the face with searching eyes.

"There's more," I said. I'd been holding it together until this point, but now the corners of my mouth stretched downwards into an ugly cry-face, and I began to sob.

Then I told her the story of Grandpa Joe.

The point is, she could have been more sensitive. Or she could have stayed more sensitive.

She started out beautifully, swearing her care for me every day, letting me know how brave and amazing I was, leaving sticky notes with affirmations on the wall above my desk. Checking on me – "Just checkin' on ya," she'd say, looking deep into my eyes and smiling. "Doin' okay?"

And she didn't want to betray my confidence, but she did make sure people in our circles knew that I was a "survivor" of some fairly gruesome shit – without getting into details, it had something to do with my childhood and molestation and a relative who was my grandfather – so they should be very careful to avoid triggering me.

"She's fragile," she'd explain to people, despite what the sticky note said (YOU ARE STRONG AND FIERCE!). Anybody who'd seen me with the scars on my upper arms exposed had already surmised that. "She's been through *a lot*." So I had celebrity and I had immunity. She cleared the way for me to act however I needed to act in any social situation.

Why, then, would she bring Miiiiiiiichael into our home, mere feet from my bed, and subject me to their vile, revolting sex? It doesn't matter that I slept through it, though *thank God* I did – waking up that morning to discover him in her bed in MY ROOM, their rank bodies entwined, was awful enough to make me start to hyperventilate, and when they didn't wake up right away, to hyperventilate louder.

As soon as I perceived movement from the bed, I rose,

retching and trembling, and stumbled into the hallway to get as far away as I could from this betrayal, this utter indifference to my mental health, this cruel, careless rubbing of my nose in their rutting. I held my arms around myself as I hurried past people, rushing towards one of the communal bathrooms, already barraged with memories I couldn't stand.

This was good, this was lucky, that I discovered who Lily truly was before getting in even deeper with her. I'd rather have known the ugly truth about someone instead of the pretty lie, even if it stabbed me in the gut; most people didn't seem to feel the same, but I'm tougher than most people. I'd lived through worse than Lily and Michael in my life. I was a "survivor."

I neglected to lock the door of the stall as I fell to my knees in front of the toilet, dry heaving with vigor. I heard Lily's voice calling my name, and I flushed before she could see how bad it had been, then struggled to my knees and over to the sink. When she opened the door, I was gripping the sides of the sink with both hands, face pale and haunted, sobbing unstoppably. I turned to her with the most wounded, abandoned, aghast face I could make.

"I'm sorry," we both said at the same time.

Even after that – with the hours of feelings-processing we had to do in order to make things even remotely okay between us, me apologizing over and over for being such a broken person and an impediment to the happy life she could lead without me, her crying and saying, "Don't say that, it's not true, I'm the one who's sorry!" – it took four hours that day before things were stable enough for her to even consider leaving the room, not because she wanted to, but in order to bring us something to eat so we could continue with the all-day, all-night talking that still needed to be done to make sure that I wouldn't kill myself for being such a pathetic, disgusting freak ("No, you're amazing, you're so important to me!") – even after all that, what does she do?

Takes Miiiiichael home for Thanksgiving instead of me.

"Remember when I said you were the only good person I ever met?" I sneered, slamming drawers in my haste to pack everything of mine so I could move out immediately and never come back. "Guess that's not true. Guess nothing about you is true."

"That's not fair," she pleaded.

Lily was worn down by the argument, which had now gone on for 48 hours, but it wasn't helping my cause. It wasn't getting her to change her mind about who she wanted to bring home. She was willing to let me think the worst of her, and she was willing to think the worst of herself whenever she thought of me, celebrating the holiday alone because my mother told me she and her husband were going to the Canary Islands over that week and I had no place else to go. She was willing to shoulder that much discomfort and cause me that much pain in order to be with her boyfriend.

I wanted to murder him. This wasn't the first time I thought about murdering someone; I've thought about murdering a lot of different people. Some murder plans have progressed farther than others in my mind. Michael's progressed all the way to the eulogy I'd give, and the sly, backhanded comments I'd plant therein for my own amusement.

The only thing holding me back was a conscience. I do have one, you know. Otherwise I'd be ten million times as bad as I am. I would gladly put a kebob skewer through Michael's heart if I thought I could live with it later.

I should have murdered Michael. He turned her against me. He started whispering to her about how I mistreated her – *I* mistreated *her*, she who'd barely been seen in our room in weeks. She, whose love for me was inexorably dimming. Everything had been idyllic before he showed up; now it was ruined. I'd gotten too angry, too possessive, taken everything too far, as usual – the mask had ripped, and she couldn't un-see what it revealed.

That's when I knew I needed to kill myself.

———

"You were in my dream," Stacy says this morning.

She is still in bed, braless and yawning and stretching, the pale ovals of her armpits winking at me. I have already shat and showered – I prefer to do both before she's awake – and I'm swaddled in my terrycloth robe, waiting for her to leave the room to pee so I can start getting dressed.

"Huh," I say.

Stacy waits, her chin tucked and her eyes upturned, for me to ask her what I was doing in her dream. It was another bad night for me, I'm frazzled, and I don't want to get into this right now, but either I flatter her or she gets pissed off. Out of all the Borderlines and Narcissists and Hysterics and Dysmorphics here, she's got to be one of the most avaricious attention-mongers this place has ever seen.

I break into a grin and leer at her. "Was I gooooooooood?"

Stacy giggles and thrashes and exudes the kind of dumbfounding, helpless-rendering cuteness baby animals emit, where your pupils grow six sizes and you moan *awwwwwww* against your will. It turns out it's not mango she smells like, it's papaya, which is even muskier and fleshier, and there is some cocoa butter in there, and maybe even some plain old butter butter, because that is what the air tastes like when she's around.

I think my sexual orientation is "cannibal."

Or maybe I'm wrong, and I am a lesbian. Maybe I am some kind of undiscovered lesbian who doesn't want to have sex but wants to be loved by every woman she meets. An emotional lesbian. But what I'm looking for is familial, not romantic, and NOT sexual. Not at all sexual; no, nothing, none, not at all, zip.

Many people assume that my aversion to sex was caused by the molestation I survived as a child. I encourage that explanation; I even subscribe to it, most of the time – it's Occam's Razor. But it bothers me that my anti-sexuality is automatically seen as a negative thing, a by-product of trauma, rather than an intrinsic strength. My lack of interest in sex is not some kind of defect or curse, it's a gift, and I'm pretty sure I've had it since birth. That's the first flaw in the molestation theory.

Second flaw: I'm not 100 percent sure if I was molested or not.

Most likely, I was. I'm 99 percent sure of it. I mean, there has to be *some* reason I am the way I am, don't you think? And not just the sex stuff, but the whole thing – you don't get as crazy as me without some serious damage done to you, right? Having a self-centered mother and no father is not a good enough reason for me to feel this desperate craving. All the literature, studies, and anecdotal evidence point to another source for this dysfunction. I had to have been molested.

I had to have been. I know I was. If I wasn't, why can I see it so clearly? Why can I feel it with every cell of my body? Any room with concrete walls makes me panic; the smell of denture cream makes me gag. And even if I did make it up, maybe without even knowing it, why did my unconscious choose those particular details to invent? Most likely because they were buried there, beaten so far underground from the force of the trauma that they had to masquerade as lies in order to surface. Something about it has to be real.

I don't know.

Sometimes I worry that I don't know what the truth is anymore. It's a little frightening sometimes, the extent to which I can put something out of, or into, my mind. I'm like a method actor. I fully inhabit the scene, experiencing everything in my stories as real: the time of day, the quality of the light, the feeling of the air on my face, how hungry I was or wasn't. When you put that kind of mental energy into creating a memory, you can't help but remember it as real.

Unfortunately, as hard as I might try, I don't ever forget what really happened and what didn't. I wish I could. I would lie to myself about Lily so hard, if I thought I could fool myself out of the truth.

I always know what happened. That's how I know I'm not crazy: I can always remember the truth of what happened. I always know what I'm doing as I'm doing it. I do it on purpose, I do it methodically, I do it aforethought and with intent. I can't plead insanity; I'm not out of my mind. I'm sane. I'm just really, really fucked up.

I would like to talk to somebody about this. Ironically, I am in a place full of people to be talked to about just this kind of thing, *id est*, what the hell is wrong with you and why you want to die. Ironically, they might even understand. Theoretically, this could end here.

Instead, I'm telling Dinah about my stepsister, my mother's former husband's daughter, who died in a car crash when I was away at summer camp one year. Her name was Lily. She was two years older than me; we were like twins.

"Right before I went away to camp," I'm saying, "we got in a big fight. She wanted to hang out with this guy, and she was supposed to come with us out to dinner that night, and instead she blew it off, and I was so mad at her for ruining the night before I went away."

Dinah nods. "That makes sense," she says. "It's upsetting, especially as you're leaving..."

She hits "leaving" with extra oomph, because leaving, for me, is particularly laden with significance. "Leaving" was what we did every four months for the first seven years of my life, then I had to "leave" and go to Florida, where... How I ever left the house after that, much less went to camp, is a miracle.

I return Dinah's nod, but it turns into me shaking my head no. I can't talk about it. I can't speak it. I can't endure reliving that last night with her. My guts contract, my throat constricts. I'm not pretending in the least.

"I just went nuts on her. I was screaming at her, 'Why is it always about you? Why can't you do one thing for me? You don't give a shit if I live or die! It's just all about you! You're so fucking selfish, and you act like you're not. You act like you give a shit about the people who love you, but all you care about is their love, not the person, not me! Fuck you!'"

I see Lily in our room, her face contorted with pain, fear in her eyes as I jab my pointed finger at her. She looks shattered, a terrified child who doesn't understand why mommy is so mad at her. I know that child. I am that child.

My fist is poised above my thigh. I want to hit somebody. The only one I'm allowed to hit is myself. I deserve it, too. I am consumed with the desire to bring down the fist, but Dinah won't accept that, so I clench it and stare at it and breath deeply, until I hear the detached part of me thinking, *This is exactly what this should look like, this gesture.* And then I know I have perspective again.

I flatten my fist and push both hands against my thighs, rubbing them back and forth, making a fire in my lap. Every muscle in my body is isometrically tensed against itself. I remember this feeling from purging. "She just...rejected me. I loved her so much..." The past tense catches in my throat. "And she loved me. We were so happy, and then it's like, she turned around and..."

This is exactly what this should look like. This agonized weeping, eyes tightly closed, shaking my head no. This is what it feels like, the time of day, the quality of the light, the feeling of the air on my face. I do it and I watch it at the same time, admiring its authenticity, because it's authentic, all right. This here – this is all me.

As awful as this is to experience, I am so grateful to find, in the middle of it, myself – my real self, the one who experiences things first hand, unshielded by construct. I wrap my arms around myself and surrender. The pain is unbearable, but it's real.

Dinah must think that I can't continue, and I can't. I don't want to. I don't want to go on and on about some fake car wreck, and the fake guilt that will never leave me (because you always have to mention how you're wracked with guilt over what you didn't do for someone who soon thereafter was *dead*).

I don't want to talk about Lily any more.

I tried to kill myself. Lily knows it, Michael knows it, everybody at school knows it. There was an ambulance, there were paramedics, there was my failure to return to campus. There was the removal of my personal items by a hired hand, so Anna and Chip didn't have to show their faces. I assume my classmates know that I didn't succeed in my attempt, but that's all they know. Nobody knows where I am now, nor will they.

"Are you still actively suicidal?" Dr. Jen asks me, in a private interview meant to determine how close I am to going home. How close am I? I'd planned to stay here a while, get a nice long rest from the outside world, but now I feel like I might need a rest from in here.

"I don't know," I say.

I'm about as suicidal as I've always been, I suppose. I continue to think about it, and not just in the usual watching-my-funeral kind of way. I'm tired. I'm in pain. Things are never going to change for me. I can't change who I am, and I can't live a lie, and this is a closet I can't ever come out of. I used to think I did the things I do for fun, or to prove something, but now I know I do it because I have to. I can't live without it. I can barely live with it.

I always say I'm going to make a fresh start, do things differently from now on. That lasts for about five seconds. I tell myself, *Well, let's think about it and see what happens and maybe I'll start doing things a little differently if it looks like that won't be too hard. Oh, okay, it's too hard. Well, I tried. Good job by me. Gonna go faint in public now.*

I don't know why I am the way I am. I don't know why everybody else isn't. I need so much, I need for at least three people, I don't know anybody who's not a junkie or paraplegic who needs as much as I do. There are villages full of half-starved children in India, and I need more than all of them combined. I need to be the most important. I need to be the most extraordinary. I need to be the most urgent priority to someone, to as many people as possible. I don't need to be famous to the world, but I need to be the biggest celebrity to everyone I know, and everybody who knows me.

People hate me for needing so much. I hate me for the same reason.

Now I'm crying again – crying when nobody's around, what a waste of tears. I'm feeling sorry for myself again. But that's good; that's how I know I have feelings. I feel sorry for myself. I feel empathy for this person, who I can see from the outside; as a viewer of the movie of my life, I think, that's not good. That's not a happy person or a successful person or a person anybody wants to be.

I can't lie enough to make the truth change. I'll never meet someone who'll know and understand me and love me as I am. Nobody will ever need me as much as I need them. I am never going to get what I want, and I am never going to be okay without it. I don't know if there's any reason to live.

Here's the worst part: I'm not suicidal. I might think about killing myself, but I'm not suicidal. I want to live. I want to live more than anybody, that's why my own one life isn't enough for me. Other people make it really goddamn difficult for me to live. But I don't want to die.

PART III

ELIZA

July 2014

8

Before After

"It almost sounds like hemophilia," says Dr. Jin.

I am reclining in my cotton gown on the crinkly paper covering Dr. Jin's exam table. I'm here to talk to her about the fatigue, the bleeding, the small cuts that fester instead of heal – I've been feeling dreadful lately. I'm very relieved to be in Dr. Jin's over air-conditioned office, nestling against the noisy paper, even if she is pressing and poking the shit out of me.

"I'd like to do a blood test," she says, frowning sympathetically. "I know that's probably the last thing you want to do right now."

"You don't have to use the needle," I suggest. "You can just get a cup and wait for my nose to start gushing."

She laughs and pats my shoulder as she goes for the supplies. She likes me. I'm a trooper. She ties me off with the rubber tube, reassuring me as she readies the needle.

"It's not hemophilia. If you had it, you wouldn't have made it to age 24 without symptoms. And there's no way you could have gotten away with that." She indicates the tattoo on my left shoulder, the one that covers my scars.

I nod. She slides the needle into the crook of my arm.

"I've only been feeling this way for a few weeks. I definitely couldn't have walked around feeling this bad my whole life."

I don't know why I want to watch this, my blood being pulled from my body. I'm actually pretty squeamish, for someone who used to slice up her shoulders and make herself puke; none of that came easily. But I'm interested in how the Warfarin is working, whether blood thinners make your blood visibly thin. I don't care if Dr. Jin finds Warfarin during the test, which she won't, because she won't be looking for it; if it does show up, I'll say, "Oh my God, I must have accidentally taken my roommates' pill! Thank you, Doctor, for catching my mistake before it killed me!"

I did, in fact, get the Warfarin from my roommate Odessa, one of five roommates with whom I share a loft in East Williamsburg. Odessa survived a pulmonary thrombosis about a year ago, and very nearly died on the L train, which I always think is going to happen anytime I ride that fucking thing anyway, especially when it stops under the East River for ten minutes while I sit there imagining the weight of all that water finally breaking through the roof of the tunnel and drowning everyone. Since her near-death scare, Odessa's lost about fifty pounds, and parades around the common space in her too-loose bras and panties, drinking vegetable juice and belching and wiping the moustache away with her forearm.

"You could also stand to gain some weight," Dr. Jin says. "You're looking undernourished in general. You're vegan, right? Are you sure you're getting enough protein?"

I'm proud of my undernourished look. It takes a lot of exercise to maintain. But she's right, I'm too thin. I'm exhausted – I've been pushing myself too hard lately – and as the blood drains from my arm, I feel woozy and afraid.

Dr. Jin eases the needle out of the vein, staunches the wound with gauze and folds my arm in on itself. The warmth of her hand is narcotic. If she could just stay right there at my side, touching my elbow, my shoulder, my cheek...

I close my eyes and start to dream about things that never happened.

I'm not going to lie: It's been a tough couple of years.

It started with the suicide attempt in junior year of high school. I was in a psych ward for a while; after that, I didn't really want to live at home anymore, not that I'd wanted to live at home before that. The middle of Florida is not known for its creative culture, its lefty politics, or its butch lesbians, all things I felt I needed in my life.

My mom didn't care if I left. All Annie cares about is couponing, staying thin, true crime TV shows, the crazy thing that happened at the salon that week, how she's down to two or three cigarettes a day now, celebrity gossip, and her younger boyfriend, Chase, as in, "to pursue in order to seize."

So I went to stay with this woman Kath in Asheville, North Carolina, an online friend who'd been encouraging me to visit her for years. Kath had just discovered she needed a mastectomy and a couple of lymph nodes removed, and she offered me room and board and spending money if I'd stay with her for a few weeks, keep an eye on the cat while she was recuperating, help her dress her wounds and reach for things on high shelves. I would have done it for free; I sincerely loved Kath, inasmuch as you can love someone you've never met. The chance to help her was the impetus for me to actually pack my bags and make arrangements to go.

Annie knew I was moving in with a woman. She'd figured out the way things were with me when I came back from the psych ward with a heart on my arm that said STACY. It had been drawn that morning in magic marker by Stacy herself, so that I would not forget her while I waited for her release. Fortunately, the marker was temporary, as was the fling.

The part my mom didn't know was that Kath was nearly forty, almost as old as she was. That would have given her pause. She might have had to ask herself, "Does my daughter want to go live with this woman as some kind of a surrogate mom? Or does she want to have a romantic relationship with this middle-aged woman?"

Or both, Annie! Or both!

Kath's first surgery appeared to have been a success, her recuperation had come along very nicely, and there were a few months, when I was first living there, when we could hardly have been happier. I didn't care if people who saw us together thought she was my mother; I enjoyed freaking people out by trying to kiss her in the supermarket. ("Cut it out," she'd say, pushing me away, but laughing. "No incest in public.")

Kath was not only my first real love affair, she was my introduction to the phenomenon of "lesbian community." I met all her friends right away in the hospital as she recuperated from surgery; it was clear that these women had mobilized to take care of Kath under the assumption that the internet chickie from Florida wouldn't pan out. Around the clock they came, day and night, a bunch of bossy, big-voiced, big-assed women, taking notes in their planners about the latest updates from the doctors: "What did the surgeon say. He didn't come by today? Who came by? The younger one? What did he say."

They stuck their hands out at me and said their names: Eileen, Mel, Pat, Bobbi, and Dinah. They weren't immediately gushing with warmth, but they weren't dicks to me either, and nobody gave me any obvious side-eye. All they wanted was for their friend to be happy – to the extent that I advanced that agenda, great. To the extent that I didn't, bye.

These strong, capable women had created a chosen family, where everyone had each other's keys, and were always going to each other's photography show or yoga class or birthday dinner, and even the ones who didn't like each other very much would still give the other a kidney (though you would *never hear the end of it* if they did – "I just think when you give someone a kidney, they should take better care of it." "I know! We all bought her that juicer and she never uses it. 'It's too hard to clean!'" "Well, now we know how she let her kidneys get so bad...").

I quickly became their favorite niece. They approved of my caretaking of Kath; they even gave me some credit for the solid, determined recovery she was making. One afternoon, I heard Mel say to Dinah regarding Kath, "Look at how happy she is. What a difference, right? Now she's got something to live *for*, not just something to live *through*."

Me. They were talking about me. It's rare that you actually overhear people talking about you when they think you're not around, even if you lurk and skulk like I do, and to hear someone say that I'd made Kath's life worth living – I couldn't have asked for a better compliment if I'd scripted it myself.

Don't get me wrong, the gals busted Kath's balls all day long about me, and as soon as I grew a pair, they busted mine, too. Our nineteen-year age difference, they noted, was a year greater than my time alive. "Hey Kath," they crowed, "You didn't tell us you wanted to have a kid by forty!"

What did we care? What we had together made us happy, whatever it was. It was definitely romantic – to me, Kath was the most interesting, perceptive, and loving person ever put on Earth, and she admired my best qualities in return – but I was sexually very shy, what with the trauma from my childhood, and Kath was physically very tired, what with the cancer and all, so it may not have been as carnal as the gals liked to make it out to be. Not quite lesbian bed death, but definitely lesbian bed rest.

The age difference did matter, after all. Kath hadn't known that I was fourteen when we met in a W4W forum; it was only after a few years, with the popularization of video chat, that I had "come out" to her as a much younger person than I'd claimed to be. She forgave me for my deception, but I knew it still weighed on her sometimes that she'd had an intimate correspondence with someone who could have landed her in prison. Even though I was no longer "jailbait," she had some mixed feelings about having corrupted a minor.

If she'd known how corrupt I was before her, she wouldn't have worried.

I was changing, though. I was cleaning up my act. I didn't self-harm anymore, I didn't even threaten to, and I used to have scads of online friends and relationships, but I was letting them all fall away. (The popularity of video chat might have had something to do with that too.) My own health has never been good, but becoming someone's caretaker must have strengthened my immune system somehow, because I had none of my chronic fainting spells or idiopathic vomiting for the first few months. I felt physically well in a way I'd never experienced before.

My mom was so envious, it hurt. It hurt her, and then she turned around and hurt me. "You sound happy," she said during one of our weekly phone calls, which were a nominal "condition" of her "letting me" go live with Kath.

"I'm happy, yeah."

"That's nice."

Her accusatory tone implied that there was only so much happiness to go around in the world, and I was having an unfair share at her expense, therefore I "owed" her some consideration, the exact nature of which she hadn't decided yet.

"How's Chase's busted knee?" I asked. Our ongoing joke was that Chase couldn't propose to her because he had a knee injury.

"I'm ready to bust his other one," she said drily.

"Let me know," I said. "I could get one of the gals here to drive down and do it for fifty bucks."

Nothing.

"Kidding," I said.

"I know." I heard her light one of her "two or three" cigarettes per day.

My mother couldn't – still can't – kid about me knowing a lot of butch women, much less about my own orientation. She's not generally homophobic; it's only me she can't stand being gay. She can't stop herself from clucking at my haircut: "At least let me put in some highlights in the front, soften it up a little."

The truth is, she can't forgive herself for what happened all those years ago with Grandpa Joe; she thinks that's what "turned" me gay. She thinks every indication of gayness on my part is an implication of her neglect and poor judgment, instead of, you know, me living my life.

That doesn't mean she's off the hook for what happened. She knows perfectly well that her shitty decisions were responsible for me enduring the same kind of abuse she suffered. It's something she "prays on" every day – not in a Jesusy-religious type of way, more in a twelve-step, self-helpy sort of way, because she got sober a number of years ago, and now she's able to "own" what happened to me. Which...no. *I* own what happened to me. *You* own a plaque with the serenity prayer on it.

I mean, I think it's great that she got sober, and that she gets to go to meetings where she can talk about all the fucked up things she did, and people applaud and call her brave and absolve her of all of it, because that was her disease that did that, and now she's Annie, and that's great. I, her teetotaling teenaged daughter, was happy to pat her head when she hit the big milestones: a month, three months, six months, a year. I listened to her try to tell me that she was sorry – it was so important to her recovery that I went to some shitty shrink's office with her to let her attempt to put words to what we'd never discussed.

Soon after that, I tried to kill myself.

She took that as another slap in her face. Because everything is about *her* face, and *her* sobriety. Fortunately Chase understands her; he's also in recovery. They met at a meeting. He was actually sober before she was, which makes no sense – he was sober, and he chose her? I think Annie wonders about that too.

Chase was another part of the reason I was "allowed" to go to Asheville – my mom was hoping he'd move in. He did, eventually, and he resides there today. I often hear him shout "Hey 'Lize," in the background of our weekly call. Still no ring, though.

Anyway. Fact is, when I was with Kath, I was demonstrably happier than my mom was, and she just seethed over it. She never asked how Kath was doing; Kath never once yelled, "Hey Annie," in the background of a phone call. When I didn't come home for Thanksgiving, Mom got miffed, as though we'd had some long-standing tradition of celebrating holidays like normal people.

"Kath is having a rough time of it. I don't want to leave her overnight."

"Well..." She struggled to think of something she could say to beat cancer. "That's your priority, I guess."

We had the same problem at Christmas, but this time I wasn't fibbing. Kath's lungs weren't working well, her liver was failing, and she had a small tumor at the base of her spine that needed immediate removal. Things went from "okay" to "not great" to "urgent" very rapidly. It was so disorienting, getting new prognoses every day. We kept thinking the pendulum was going to swing back the other way and we'd go back to where we'd been on December 2, the day before she started to cough.

By New Year's, everything had gone so far south it was Antarctic. The spinal surgery had not gone well, she had not recovered from it, and her friends and I were keeping a vigil at the hospital, sleeping on each other's shoulders in hard-armed chairs. We became familiar with the other cliques of visitors in the Intensive Care waiting room – the yentas with the dying sister, the large Indian-American family with the dying grandmother – we went from nodding to smiling to asking how the other's person was doing, then back to smiling, but sadly, and not asking.

I rarely and unwillingly surrendered my spot in Kath's room, perching on the radiator by the head of her bed because the space was too narrow for a chair, and I needed to be right there with her. I had not said anything like, "In case this is goodbye…" because that's shitty etiquette when someone's on their way to surgery, so it looked like I might have to tell her now:

Kath, you saved my life. You started saving it all those years ago, when you emailed me to see how I was doing because you hadn't seen me around the boards. I know I've told you this a million times, but you still don't know what that did for me. It was such a bad time, I was being extra bullied at school, Annie was still drunk, and the day I got the email from you I was about to send an order to a Canadian pharmacy for enough Vicodin to get me to comatose, if not all the way to dead, but I knew it was worth staying alive a little bit longer if there was a chance of feeling the way your email made me feel again. I already admired you so much from what you'd posted, you were such a beloved presence to everyone, and the more I got to know you, the less I could believe how lucky I was to be your friend.

The last few months have been the best of my life. They've made up for all the years that came before them, because those are the years that led me to you. If I hadn't met you, I'd be dead. And I don't want to live without you now. But I'm not going to waste the love you gave me by throwing it away, having watched you fight so hard to live. I'm going to try to repay you by having the best life I can, and thinking of you and loving you every day, and keeping you alive inside me.

Kath lived another eight days, never regaining consciousness. Then we all went back to her house and started packing it up. There was nobody to pay the next month's rent, and no reason to. Dinah had already adopted the cat; now she picked me up too.

After that came the period I refer to as "my lost years." I stayed with Dinah for a few weeks, then moved out to Oakland to be with someone I met online; she and I wound up doing a lot of drugs. Speed, molly, coke, LSD. The Vicodin I hadn't bought all those years ago. One time on LSD I had the most terrifyingly candid mental conversation with myself. Like, *We are not who we say we are, we know that, right? We've created this construct that we call a self, but that's not at all what's inside us, is it. And now we're trapped, aren't we.*

I stopped taking LSD after that. Drugs are supposed to drown that shit out, not force you to listen.

It was an intense scene. We knew a lot of bartenders and sex workers – that was all we knew – all of them competing to be the toughest and most badass. The North Carolina gals would have shit some kiln-fired bricks if they knew what I was up to, which was getting fucked up out of my mind and having a bunch of sex I was grateful I couldn't remember the next day. Dinah was sending me money for a while, because I was having trouble "getting on my feet" in the aftermath of Kath's death. If I ever did the twelve-step thing, Dinah would've been first on my list of amends.

But since my mother had already ruined twelve-step by getting her grubby mitts all over it, I had to get sober by myself.

I might as well skip over the two years before my sobriety. I wish I'd been able to skip it the first time.

I was twenty-two and temporarily residing in Eugene, Oregon, sponging off someone else I met online, when I woke up one morning and realized, *I can't do this any more.* I had some kind of fungal infection on my arms and legs and torso, it was spreading between my toes and the webbing of my fingers. It rained so goddamn much there, I was red and itchy and mildewed, rickety from lack of sun, and on this particular morning, I felt like I'd been drinking from the mostly-empty beer bottles with cigarette butts in them that were ubiquitous at our place, unstoppable in their proliferation, so why even try to keep up.

I hadn't been calling home much. When I did, Annie said she

needed to let me do what I needed to do. She certainly wasn't going to put up with any addict behavior in her home, nor was she going to fund that kind of behavior for me someplace else, but if I wanted to do something like enroll in community college, or go to trade school, she would pay for it. "Not an apartment, not a phone, not anything, except something so you can get your life together."

I borrowed this girl's bike and rode around for a while, trying to figure out what to do. It felt like a good idea to ride the hell out of the bike, to try to tire the bike out like a puppy, to tax my legs and my lungs and my heart, push out all the toxins in my body at once. After I did that, and then vomited a few times, I went back to the house, drank my weight in water, got online and put out an SOS: Need sober environment quickly, will repay in gratitude immediately and money eventually.

The next morning, I was on my way to Vancouver.

I called in sick to work this morning.

One of the great things about working for a national chain: They always have enough employees to call in a sub for you without too much trouble. I don't give a shit about my co-workers, but I do give a shit about not pissing people off by leaving the store short-handed. If my illness makes things harder for others, they're way more likely to squawk about it; as it is, the only one who really loses is me, and it's only a day's pay, which I can easily make up for with extracurricular activities.

Another great thing: stellar health coverage. I get to go to as many doctors as I want – I mean, as many doctors as I *need* – and Human Resources has to make as many allowances for my varying conditions as possible. Lawsuits aren't my game, but my corporate bosses don't know that. All they know is that I'm mysteriously sick a lot, and have been working with various medical specialists to try to diagnose the issue.

To begin today's sick day, I do my full workout (three mile run, twenty-five push-ups, one hundred crunches, up and down the stairs of our building five times, then a bunch of squats, lunges, burpees, and tricep dips, finished off with a minute and a half of plank). My favorite game at house parties is getting someone to call me skinny and challenge me to some kind of physical bet, so I can drop to the floor and bang out push-ups like they're nothing, thus increasing my circle of groupies.

Around lunchtime, I head over to the Collective to see who's around. Most of my friends work there, but I was fired for sicking out too often – who would have guessed that corporate America cares more about its employees' health than the lesbian-feminist coffee shop-bookstore does?

Whatever; it's way better that I don't work there with everybody. They're all sick of each other because they're up each other's asses all the time. I used to get jealous, after I was first fired, when I would come in and see everyone in Collective mode, making their jokes and having their day and being a non-hierarchical team, and I knew how tight that made them, these friendships that were forged in battle, and I wasn't part of it anymore. What I didn't realize was how much more attractive I was when I made myself scarce.

"'Lize!"

At least three people say my name as I come in, then greet me separately:

Desia: "What's up, baby?"

Sabrina: "How are you?"

C.J.: "Where you been?"

I hug and kiss and pound them, as appropriate, then answer to all, "I'm all right, how's things here?" I like to reinforce the idea that they cease being individuals when they're at work – it *is* a collective, after all – and they are all one person to me while they're here, an undifferentiated blob of friend. Meanwhile, I breeze in and out, on no fixed schedule; I hit them with a bunch of new anecdotes, ask a few questions, then leave 'em wanting more.

Emotional Economics 101: Scarcity adds value. When a commodity is scarce, people are inclined to pay more for it, wait longer for it, and choose to purchase it more quickly. I didn't realize it before – all my life, all I knew how to play was the very short game of *gimme now*, where anything except everything is unacceptable and more is never enough – but in many cases, you can get closer to people and mean more to them if you interact with them less.

Lila pipes up, unsolicited, from her position at the sink. "How come you're not working today?"

She is inimitably top-to-toe Lila right now – no surprise, because Lila is always Maximum Lila. She's doing her '50s pin-up thing, with a kerchief tied around her hair, so she looks like the We Can Do It lady from the World War Two posters. Because she's a regular Rosie the Riveter, she is; that's how hard Lila works and how seriously she takes this job, as well as everything else in her life. You'll note that she is not looking up from rinsing glasses while asking why I'm there, because the rinsing needs to be done *right now* while everyone else apparently is just going to stand around and talk to me; also so that the vigorous spattering of water will drown us out.

"Hi, Lila." Good to see you too.

What's funny is, Lila and I are close friends. She let me stay at her place when I first got to town, and we still hang out and text each other, though not as much as we used to before she was forced to raise the issue of my firing at the Collective meeting a couple of months ago because nobody else was going to do it.

Lila glommed on pretty hard to me as soon as I came around last year, and I admit, I let her. It was appealing, having this tall, substantial, maternal woman who wanted to fix me hanging around. I'd been mooching off women kind of like her for the past two or three years; I knew what a cushy set-up it could be, minus the fixing part.

Lila also very helpfully acted as my envoy to the rest of the group, letting them know the tragedy of what had happened with Kath and telling them the few grizzly details of my non-sober years I let slip.

"I haven't actually talked about this stuff with anybody," I confessed, as she sat behind me and rubbed my shoulders on her couch. Subtext: You're different than other people. You're special. I don't trust anybody, but I trust you. "Weird, huh."

You know what works a lot like scarcity? Abstinence. Unannounced abstinence, to be sure – in the same way I don't announce my sobriety, for fear of making people feel weird drinking around me, I don't say anything about being abstinent.

I just don't have sex. I'll flirt with you – Jesus, I'll flirt with you until your ears come, but I'll always let you know I'm not being serious, and at the end of the night, I'm going back to the loft nobody has ever seen, with the roommates nobody has ever met, alone.

I've been called a tease, a cad, and worse. When girls ask about me, they're told, *Don't even bother; she'll suck you in and spit you out.* That's not entirely true. I wouldn't say that I seduce and then reject people. I would say that I let people as far in as I can afford to have them there, I make a valid attempt to participate in bonding, then I make them aware that my psychological and emotional difficulties render it impossible for me to do anything that might upset the delicate balance of my sanity, such as have sex or enter a relationship with them.

Which makes it convenient for me to dismiss people as "pissed that I didn't want to sleep with her." Lila looks like she'd fit that category right now, like a woman spurned, except it's not her body I'm spurning, it's her *heart*, and that's even more hurtful.

Good. Let her stew, that sanctimonious hag. Why aren't I at work? Because I don't have to be. Sorry you do! Sucks to be you. What do you care anyway? You want to call a meeting at the corporate office so you can raise the issue of firing me?

She didn't know the favor she did me by getting me fired, but I think she's catching on.

"I'm actually between doctor's appointments."

"What are they saying?" Desia asks, concerned. Desia is even newer to the group than I am, and she's very solicitous, but before I can answer, she goes to help a customer.

"Are you getting anything?" asks Lila. "If not, you have to make way in front of the counter there."

I ask for a chai tea. Chai tea makes me think of Kath. I have a flash of being with her that November, all those many years ago; nothing cinematic or specific, just a general "Oh, Kath" moment. She existed, now she's gone. This happens every time I smell chai tea.

"Is that it? You want to eat something for a change?"

Desia shoots me a sympathetic look from her register, like, *God, Lila, stop trying to be everyone's mom.* Anytime she's not around, that's the first thing everyone says about her: "Lila *has* to stop being such a mommy." But nobody says it to her face, and they all go along with the act; they allow her to nickname them, they baby talk with her, and when they need to borrow money, they turn to Lila. Then they turn around and criticize her for it.

For everyone we hang out with, there's a first thing people say about her. "She *has* to dump her girlfriend." "She *has* to stop with the OCD anal-retentive shit." "She is such a *martyr* all the time." "She just talks your ear off, and she never even, like, *pauses*."

We all do it to each other, and we all watch the others do it to everybody else, yet people don't seem to realize, *this happens first thing every time I walk out of the room.* They all say something about me that none of them would ever say to me.

I wish everybody would just say it. It would change everyone's lives so much for the better if we all said to each other, "We voted, and here's what's wrong with you." I'm dying to know the first thing people say about me when I'm not around. I don't think I've ever heard a first thing about someone I know that I disagreed with.

If I could choose my own first thing people say about me, it would obviously be, "I'm worried about her." As in, "She carries such a heavy burden, as we all know, and she's so brave about it, and she won't admit it's wearing her down because she has to be the tough guy all the time, but we should really collectivize and intervene, sit her down and tell her how much we all love her, and let her know that we've come up with a plan to take care of her for the rest of her life."

But I'll settle for, "I'm worried about her." And if anybody wants to accuse me of not eating enough, or of having exercise anorexia, I'll take that too. My sexual dysfunction – because you must be "dysfunctional" if you don't feel like having sex all the time – you can go ahead and dissect that behind my back all you want, it's fair game. It's all part of the image.

Here's what I dread my first thing is: "She's so manipulative. She's so full of shit. She's so obvious, and she thinks she's so smart. You can't ever believe a word she says. She's so conceited. I am embarrassed for her. Let's all imitate her unkindly now."

I say to Lila, "I would get a salad, but..."

But wouldn't you prefer to give it to me for free? Wouldn't that make you feel like the most generous, patient person? Wouldn't it prove to everyone once and for all that you are right about everything when you tell me how I should live my life, and I should listen to you? You always know the right thing to do, Mama Lila.

She sighs and rolls her eyes. "I'll put some of the quiche on there. But you have to promise to eat it, because it's really good." She assembles the order and brings it all back. I have the money for the chai tea in my hand, but she waves it away. She'll pay for it with her discount.

"Thank you," I say, quietly and humbly, leaning in so it's just between me and her, full eye contact. "I really do appreciate you, Liles." I don't mean to be a cocky asshole, I just can't show vulnerability with others around, because I am insecure.

"Don't eat and leave," she says. "I want to talk to you."

I tense up a little, bracing myself before I nod yes, because I know what she wants to say: She is worried about me.

"IT'S JUST, LILA REALLY CARES ABOUT YOU A LOT, AND IT UPSETS HER WHEN YOU DON'T TAKE CARE OF YOURSELF."

This girl Christine is yelling at me over the noise of the bar where we're assembled for our friend Maria's birthday drinks.

To be fair, Christine would probably be yelling even if it weren't noisy. Christine has a lot of confidence in what she says, its importance to you, and your desire to hear it at length right away, even if there's a very interesting, enigmatic fortyish woman leaning against the wall, alone, watching everything going on around her with a slight smile.

"I KNOW."

"LILA HAS INVESTED A LOT OF HER TIME AND ENERGY INTO YOU, AND..."

Blah blah blah. I nod, stand up, and clap Christine on the shoulder as I wiggle away, the clap meaning, *Thanks, Sport, for taking the time to talk to me about this. I won't admit it, but I needed it. You've helped me see things in a new light.* Then I take my club soda and go stand over by the wall.

"I TRIED TALKING TO HER," I hear Christine yell at Lila. "SHE NEVER LISTENS."

I smile at the mystery woman. "That's me she's bellowing about."

"Sorry?" she asks, leaning closer and turning an ear my way. Is that a motherfucking British accent? Because I will die down dead if it is. I try not to like things everybody else likes, but come on, British accents.

"Oh, sorry. I thought you overheard something..."

"Ah," she says, looking straight ahead and nodding.

She's not interested. Why would she be? She's obviously very cool, very content being alone, doesn't need the companionship of a twenty-four year old part-time customer service associate/ full-time headcase to enjoy her evening. I like what she's wearing: grey t-shirt, dark selvage jeans. You can tell by the drape that it's all high quality stuff. I'd be all right with looking like her when I'm old.

I saunter away, back to the group, and Maria, the birthday girl, catches me by the arm.

"Granny chaser," she says, shoving me. I pretend to stumble from the force of her push.

Out of all the girls, Maria is the one I'm closest to, and the one I've come closest to being with. We hit it off as soon as I started coming around the Collective, and after I was done with Lila, Maria and I became one of those will-they-or-won't-they friend-couples, about whom everyone says, "Why don't you two just do it and shut up, already?"

Then one night we went back to her place after a dinner party, and I started getting ready to sleep over, as was customary, and she said, "I can't sleep next to you anymore unless we're together." And when I realized she was serious, I put my shirt, pants, and sneakers back on and walked out without another word.

It was kind of a big deal – we didn't contact each other for a few weeks, and avoided seeing each other in public, while everyone sat around agreeing that I was the bad guy in this scenario. It was obvious to all that I was too fucked up to be with someone as awesome as Maria. Christine, Maria's long-ago ex, had been eating her heart out over our friendship; now she was adamant that I was not good for Maria. I was a mindfuck, I was a little girl who played a lot of games, and Maria needed to "protect herself" better.

Soon after that, I had one of my first bad bleeds and wound up in the ER. Maria came right away, Lila in tow.

"I love you, you asshole," Maria told me, leaning over my bed and gripping the hand that didn't have the IV in it. "You don't get to die unless I kill you."

Since then, everybody's been just peachy with each other. Maria and I are back to being good friends (though not as close as before), Lila stopped resenting Maria as much and now *they're* good friends, and Christine continues to think I give a flapping fuck about what she has to say to me. Which is why it now falls to her to tell me how I should treat Lila.

But she can take a break from that, because here comes Lila herself, bearing down on me. "You," she says, and pulls me away from Maria to stand with her in the corner.

"Me," I say.

"I know you're avoiding me because you don't want to hear what I have to say." She has her fists on her hips, like she's the principal of our clique and I'm a naughty student. "That's why I'm not going to take it personally."

I start grinning a little. That's what I do when I'm nervous, I inappropriately grin and then try to suppress it. Kind of like a tic, but on purpose. That way everyone can tell when I'm nervous and I'm trying to hide it. So when I'm actually nervous, they can't tell, because I'm not trying to suppress a weird grin.

I'm told that I'd be terrible at poker.

"You know that I love you," Lila says. "Stop grinning. I do. I'm sorry it makes you so uncomfortable to hear that, but...deal with it."

"I care about you too, Liles."

She rolls her eyes. "Whatever. We need to have a *serious* talk."

"Are we doing this now? I may require a few more club sodas before I can handle this."

(Translation: You drink alcohol, Lila, and I don't, but I'm not lecturing you on anything, am I. So enjoy feeling weird about that, hypocrite.)

"No, yeah, we need to do this now."

I sneak a peek behind me. Everybody's watching, pretending not to watch. I let this register on my face as frustration and embarrassment. They know I hate being the center of attention. "Fine." I cross my arms. Oppositional defiant. "Can we at least step outside?"

I indicate with a sweep of my hand that she should go first out the door, because that's the chivalric code: whiny bitches first. As I follow her outside, I look pointedly away from the rest of the group. How dare they all talk about me, hopefully a lot. The second the door swings shut, they'll start saying the first thing they always say.

Lila leans a shoulder against the building. "Eliza, if you need help, you have to ask for help."

"All three syllables," I note. "I'm in trouble."

"Please don't fucking kid around with me. Please don't blow me off. I'm saying please, okay?" She's so frustrated, she's near tears. "Listen to me without talking for one minute, okay? It's not funny."

I "try to suppress my grin so she doesn't see it and guess at the true feelings behind it."

"I'm sorry," I say. "I'm nervous." I stop grinning and look serious, then cast my gaze downward and nod at the sidewalk for the part that's difficult for me to admit. "You're right. I've been afraid to hear what you have to say, but I need to hear it, and I'm grateful that you give enough of a shit about me to want to say it, and I'm not being sarcastic, okay? I'm sorry. I'm sorry I've been a dick. I want to hear what you have to say."

Her expression immediately softens. Man, she is *good* at giving this kind of talking-to; it's already working so well. Let me tell you, if someone needs to be set straight, Lila's your gal. She starts in, still naggy and pedantic, but a good fifty percent less so.

"I don't even think you know how much people care about you. Nobody wanted you to get fired, *I* didn't want you to get fired..."

"Liles, that was months ago, we're all good with that."

"No, we're not. I'm not good with it." She's getting flustered again, losing her place. She expected to get in two solid minutes of whatever angry monologue she's been prepping in her head before I started agreeing with her. Now she's taken a left turn into feeling guilty because she got me fired from the Collective and I forgave her. "I'm really mad that you gave us all no choice, and then *I* had to be the bad guy and bring it up, of course, but that's..." She gestures with her head in the direction of the bar. "A whole 'nother thing."

Now she's remembering that she's frustrated with the rest of the girls, who always make her do the heavy lifting; nobody else was going to step up and say what needed to be said unless she did it, just like right now. So unfair, says the look on her face. Why is *she* always the one who has to be the stern parent, when she really wants to be the rebellious teenaged daughter, getting shitfaced and cutting loose with me and dancing until her skirt has migrated around her waist so that the zipper is over on her left hip? And then going back to her place and crying to me about how put-upon she is while I hug her around the back, spoon-style?

That actually sounds fine right about now. Go back to Lila's place, which is suspiciously well-appointed for a collectivist barista's; watch some TV, kid around, spoon. I haven't had any spoon in weeks.

"Do you want to get out of here and talk about it?"

She gives me an odd look, like she's thrown by the question. "Um," she says. "I feel like I need to say this now."

"Okay." I take a deep, noisy breath in. "Hit me. I mean, don't *hit* me..."

"It's not cute anymore, 'Lize. You turn everything into a joke, and it's not a joke. I know you never want to be serious about anything, but sometimes you have to be a grown-up. Like, take some responsibility in your life. I was so pissed at you the other day – I *knew* you were supposed to be at work – and I *know* you had doctors, but you can't miss any more days there or you're going to get fired, just like...."

"What am I supposed to..."

She raises her voice to cut me off. "You have to schedule your appointments around work. That's how it's done in the real world."

I bite my lip, another gesture people make when they're uncomfortable, and re-cross my arms. "Okay...so you're mad at me because I skipped work for a doctor's appointment that I only got at the last minute because she had a cancellation, and I'm supposed to say, 'Oh no, I have to work, I'll wait another two weeks?' Because the sooner I see her, the sooner..."

"Okay, I know. And I want the full update on what she had to say. But I want you to listen to me first."

But now I'm all het up. Lila's really getting to me now! "Why do you care if I get fired, anyway? I don't work with you anymore."

"Because! It shows that you're going to keep doing the same things! You have to stay employed! Because I can't support you anymore, and nobody else can support you either. I mean, you come in to the store today, you didn't go to work, you look exhausted, you don't have any money..."

"I had money! I was trying to buy a tea! I had the money out for the tea and you wouldn't take it!"

(NB: Absolutely true, as you'll recall. I didn't ask her for free tea, I didn't ask her for a free salad, and I never even said the word "quiche." She elected to give all that to me. One of the first rules of mooching: never ask for what you want. Allow someone else to offer it. I know she went out of pocket eight bucks for me, but she offered it. And she offered it because she wanted to, she can afford to, and it made her feel good. She bought some moral carbon credits to bank against any angry feelings she might have towards me later.)

"I'm tired of feeling like I have to look out for you because you won't do it yourself. Your health is awful..."

"That's not my fault! I'm seeing so many fucking doctors, and they all say different things, and nobody gives me any answers." Now I am near tears. I let them collect and shine in my eyes. "I want to be healthy, I do."

"Then you have to eat more food. Okay? And maybe you can't do a million push-ups every day. Maybe you can't run around to everybody's birthday things and whatever, because you need to let yourself rest..."

"Should I not be here tonight?"

"Eliza, stop it." This is the monologue she's been planning to deliver; now's her chance. "Look, I'm only going to say this once. You have to take better care of yourself. Whatever you're doing is not working. It's not. And it's not fair to the people who love you. We're all worried about you, you're obviously having a really hard time, and we don't want that for you. I don't want to have to come see you in the ICU ever again. Because that was awful, okay?"

Lila chokes up. She's not even exaggerating. She's starting to cry over this. "That was so frightening. If you'd lost any more blood you would have been dead. And if you died? I don't know what the fuck I would do. Because that's how much I love you. I love you so much."

Ahhhhhhhhhhhhhhhhh.

There it is. She means it, too. She loves me. I embrace her, and the love comes off her in waves of manifest energy. I absorb it with every cell.

Ahhhhhhhhhhhhhhhhhhhhhhhhhhhhhhhhhhhhhhhhhhhhhhh.

Lila breaks down and starts weeping, really sobbing from the body. I embrace her tighter. "I'm sorry," I say into her hair. "I'm so sorry. Liles, you're right, I've been an asshole. I don't ever want to make you worry. You are such a good person, and you're so important to me."

She sobs and sobs. She's got her arms wrapped around herself, and I'm wrapped around that, but when I release her far enough to look at her full in the face, to let her see what effect her love has on me, she lets me pull her back in without the crossed arms. She cries for another minute, while I croon to her.

"Thank you. Thank you, Liles. I mean it. You're right about everything. I mean, not everything..." She laughs, snuffles. "Don't quote me on that." Her arms crawl around my back, the hug gets tighter. Full frontal spoon. "You are such a good person. You are so important to me."

We sway back and forth like the old couple that's still on the dance floor at the end of the wedding party. Her crying is winding down. Now she's crying more out of relief than anything else – she was *so* frustrated, and now she is *so* relieved, and the intensity is overwhelming. It feels like an orgasm, to cry like that, or so they tell me.

"I am really afraid they're going to fire me," I confess. "And I can't lose my insurance right now. I know I need to just concentrate on working and getting healthy...seriously, you're right. I should be home right now trying to force my body to make more blood. I should be eating nothing but steaks. I'm not kidding! I'm not even being facetious. Dude, I'm taking this totally seriously." I let my voice gravel a little. "It means so much that you care about me enough to say this. It's so good for me, knowing someone loves me enough to care if I'm alive or dead."

"Everybody loves you. *Everybody* loves you. You don't even know."

I let her go again, our arms still entwined, but with enough room between us that she can see my soft, truly smiling face. "You know you're the one who matters, though. You know...I love you too."

I don't say those words very often, not even in a friend way. I don't bandy them about the way some folks do. Scarcity theory again. Lila closes her eyes and lets her forehead touch mine.

"You know I love you," I say again. "Because I wouldn't take this shit from anybody but you."

She laughs. She feels incredible. She has had so many different chemicals coursing through her body in the last ten minutes – the adrenaline of confronting me, the serotonin of relief, the oxytocin of being held and told you're loved. Her face is flushed like she's been running towards me for blocks.

I embrace her again, then let her go. I dip my chin and look right into her eyes. "But listen – you need to concentrate on yourself more too. You know? No, listen – you're always taking care of other people; you know you are. You give everybody so much, and we all take it for granted because you're Lila, and that's who you are, and you couldn't stop being you because that's how big your heart is. But who takes care of you, when you're taking care of everyone else? You know? Missy? Who's taking care of you, hmmm? You should take some of your own advice sometime, it's good stuff."

We are so close together, and she looks so pretty right now. The scowl she's been working doesn't suit her face; she was meant to look like she does right now: mouth slightly open and smiling, eyes rinsed of stupid makeup, adoration and gratitude shining in them. Hair a little messy, like a human woman and not a kewpie doll. I could kiss her right now. But I don't.

We go back inside the bar, arms around each other, and I give a sheepish wave to the crew. "Good chat," I say, back to pretending to be too tough for feelings, even though everyone clearly sees that deep feelings were felt deeply out there on the sidewalk.

Christine ignores me and approaches Lila, a drink in hand meant for her. "Thanks, Sweetie," says Lila, beaming. Well, will you look at that: Christine's taking care of Lila.

"Come here," says Christine, leading her away, giving me a quick but extremely evil eye. Lila smiles apologetically as she goes. I hear Christine ask, "How'd it go?"

Maria asks me the same thing. "You two have a good talk?"

I slide in to the bench seat. "Yeah, you know. She's...she just cares about me, that's all."

"Looked pretty caring from in here." She indicates the front window, through which Lila and I had been partly visible. "Christine almost ran out there at the end."

"Why does Christine ca...OH." For someone so supposedly smart and keen and perceptive, I am an idiot. I can't believe I missed the fact that Christine and Lila are hooking up. "OHHHHHHH."

That's why Lila didn't want to go talk at her place. She's going home with her new girlfriend tonight. WOW. I'm having a hard time reconciling myself with this. Christine and Lila. The fact that I missed it feels like an especially bad sign, like I'm slipping, and that freaks me out. Something is very askew here. Not sure what planet we're supposed to be on right now, but it's not Earth, because Lila's picking Christine over me, and there is no way that could be happening there.

See, now, this is the drawback of my scarcity game. I'm out of the loop. I've been hanging back too much; I see that now. I need to regain focus. And I may need to accelerate my timeline – I'm not the only one who's slipping. Lila didn't remember to ask me again how the doctor's visit went before we came inside.

Now Christine's going to keep her at the other end of the

bar for the rest of the night. No more happy hugging, no more cuddly feelings. That's too bad. Lila and I were having a special time together. I was remembering how comfortable I could be in her company. I must be staring in their direction, because Maria nudges me with her leg.

"Jealous?" she asks.

"Never." I kick back and stretch out.

This feeling is not jealousy. It is insane rage. Christine is a hag from hell, that smug, ugly, pathetic *bloody hatchet wound*. And now she's going to try and get in between me and Lila, the way she tried – TRIED – to do with me and Maria? And then, on top of that, she's going to tell me how I should behave towards my friend? Please, bitch. You are nothing. I am a dynamic, multilayered, fascinating enigma. You are the menu at a chain restaurant.

"You?" I ask.

"Not much." Maria's looking over there, probably wondering how she missed it too. I know she's as baffled as I am. *But...we're the more objectively desirable ones here. We're the ones that get chased; they're supposed to be the chasers.* Whether we want them or not, we want them to remain ours.

Maria and I understand each other in a lot of ways. It really *was* fun, shacking up with Maria part time for a while there.

She hits my leg with hers again.

"Quick," she says. "Let's make out."

9

Attention Benefit Disorder

I'm at work the next day when I get a message from Annie. I would transliterate all of her dialogue here to give you the full Floridian-ness of it, but it would become unreadable immediately, and is also Collectively incorrect – we don't make fun of people for their Southern or "hick" accents; it's classist. So we'll just say that the message begins with, "Hah, 'Layz!" and we'll leave it at that.

The content of the message is even more disturbing than the accent in which it is delivered: Annie and Chase are coming to New York. Chase is representing his wholesale kitchenware company at a trade show; they will be here in two weeks for three days. My mom doesn't like to give me a lot of notice on things like this, so she can catch me in the act of living my life.

I call her back a few hours later, when I get home. "Hey, Mom."

We're back to talking once a week these days – not for long, just five or ten minutes. Just so she can hear my voice, tell me her latest news, and confirm for herself that "you're alive and doing all right." It's been a year and a half since I got sober, and I have no temptation to drink or use, but she doesn't know that, and neither do my friends, who give me an attaboy every time I quietly mention, "I have two years sober today – don't tell everyone, I don't want it to be a big deal."

Or, "For some reason, I was having the worst craving to get totally shitfaced yesterday. I was at work, and it hit me out of nowhere, the urge to leave right then and go straight to the bar on the corner, which, obviously I wasn't going to do. But then it kept nagging at me all day, 'I could go to the bar as soon as I'm done here.' 'Only two more hours to go, then I could go to the bar.' I could see the whole thing, I could feel the bills in my hand, I could taste the whiskey, I could feel it burn on the way down, then the knockout punch, you know? Where it's like, 'Oh yeah, I felt that. It's *on* now.' And I was telling myself, 'Well, I'm sober right now, so whatever decisions I make when I'm sober are going to be responsible ones, so this is okay.' Isn't that fucking crazy? I know.

"I have to say, it freaked me out; I haven't had a craving like that since I cleaned up. I really thought I was past all that. I mean, how many times have I hung out with you while you're drinking, and I've been completely fine?

"But yeah, yesterday I came way too close, I mean, right up until the last minute as I was leaving work, putting on my coat and scarf, putting on my bag – the whole time I was like, 'I'm going to do it. I'm definitely going to do it.' And I'm asking myself, 'Wait, why am I going to do this? This isn't something I can undo. Why would I do this?' And all I can hear in my head is, 'Fuck you, shut up, because I want to.'

"So obviously, I didn't do it, you know; I practically ran down the street to the subway, and I was pacing back and forth on the platform like, 'This train better get here *now*.' And then I realized, I'm thinking if I can avoid walking past this one bar, I'll be fine, like there aren't twelve more bars on every block. It was bad times, dude, I basically ran home and got into bed and curled into a ball for the rest of the night. I'm okay now, but...I don't know. That was almost a little bit scary. I guess I've been under more stress than I realized. Oh, hey, and please don't say anything about this to Lila, I don't want her to worry. I'm okay now. For now."

Attaboy!

My mother, by the way, is so sober that she's somebody else's sponsor now. That she is seen as qualified to help someone through one of the lowest times in their lives is mindboggling – when Kath was in a coma, and we were all basically living at the hospital, she said a number of jaw-droppingly selfish things to me, e.g., "I know your friend is in the hospital, but you can still pick up the phone," and, "You've only known her a few months, anyway." But hey, she's not my sponsor.

Still smoking cigarettes, too, as I can clearly hear.

"Chase is going to be busy during the days, but – *mmmph* – I'm free."

A strange thought occurs: What if she deliberately smokes over the phone so I can hear her, just to see if I'll say anything about her "two or three cigarettes a day" bullshit? What if everything she says and does is some kind of test to see if I'm paying attention?

"I have to work those three days."

"You can't switch with someone? Even for one day?" She is "plaintive," mere consonants away from "complainy."

"I'm working as many shifts as I can right now. I have to make up for a bunch of days I missed."

(Pause.)

(Why did you miss a bunch of days of work, Eliza? Is everything okay? Are you feeling better since that last illness? How's your sobriety going? I'm concerned for you.)

"Not even *one day*?" she says.

No wonder I do what I do.

"I can't. And I seriously hope you have a hotel room, because there's no way all three of us can fit in my room, plus there's my whole roommate situation..."

"Of course we have a hotel room! But I do want to see where you live in your loft apartment. It's in Brooklyn, right? Williamsburg is in Brooklyn? Mallory about died when I told her – she said, 'It's all black people in Brooklyn!' I said, 'Mallory, honey, you need to get out and see the world. I mean, go to Miami, even.'"

Because of her twelve-step group, my mother now has "black friends," who she is eager to describe as "plenty" and not much more. And now she is so much less racist than everybody else! If she times it right, she could add two of my roommates to the long list of "plenty of black friends" she has talked to *once in her life*. By the time she gets back from New York, she is going to be so post-racial, she'll have to navigate traffic by relying on spatial memory, because Annie doesn't care if a stoplight is red or green or even purple, color doesn't make a difference to her, it's what's inside that stoplight that matters!

"I promise you'll see people of all skin tones and persuasions," I say.

"And we want to meet your friends, too."

Whoa, no. No no no no no.

"Yeeeah..." No. No. No. No. "But...everybody's kind of working a lot, they're busy with their own... I don't know if I can, like, logistically..."

She cuts in. "Is there some reason you don't want me to meet the people you spend time with?" *Hmmmm?*

I love it when my mom decides she needs to police me to make sure I'm not hanging out with a bunch of junkies and speed freaks. I love that she's pulling the "I'm your mother, I want to meet your friends" bit. Like she's not going to let me have friends she doesn't approve of. I don't need her permission to have friends. I'm twenty-four years old. What power does she have over me; what's she going to do, stop calling me? That'd be fine, don't call me. Then I can stop cowering.

"I don't even think anybody's going to be around," I say weakly.

"Mmmph." Is she lighting another smoke? She's fucking with me on purpose now, she wants to see if I have the balls to say something. "So, what...so you think I want to embarrass you? I don't want to embarrass you in front of your friends. I don't want you to be embarrassed by us." She is on the cusp of self-righteousness, but she wisely pulls back on that. "Just introduce us to at least one person in your life, all I'll say is hi and goodbye."

"We'll see." No. Not a chance.

Self-righteous again: "That's not too much to ask. Most people don't make such a big deal out of their friends meeting their parents."

Oh, Annie. Too far.

"Are we going to talk about most people now?" I am ready to throw down. I am always ready to throw down with her, and I love that she gave me the opening. She just "blew her chance" to meet "my girlfriend." I emit a harsh laugh. "I'm not sure either you or I are 'most people.'"

"Okay, you're right, never mind." She backs right off. She is not ready to throw down tonight, in which case she needs to get rid of that super-irritating backing-away-from-a-grizzly-bear voice. "I'm sorry. I don't want to push you too hard. I don't want to argue."

Then don't start fights! "I don't want to argue either. Don't make it out like I'm making you argue, I don't want to argue with you."

I don't want to argue with her, and furthermore I shouldn't have to, because we should both be firmly agreed that she's lucky I have any contact with her at all, considering our past together, much less a friendly relationship that sometimes verges on the daughterly.

I bring my voice back down. "I don't want to argue either. I'll try to put something together with some friends or something. It might not happen, but...."

"That'd be so great! I promise I won't say anything to anybody, just 'hello' and 'nice to meet you.' Oh, honey, I can't wait to see your loft apartment. If you want, Chase and I can pick you up from your job one night, and we can all go get some steaks in Times Square." She pauses for response. "Kidding," she says.

I go from hating her to laughing with her to hating myself for laughing with her. "Okay, Maaaaa." I bleat it like a goat. "I got to go wash my face and stuff, but we'll talk more before you get here."

I wait for her to say she loves me. She waits for me to say the same.

"Okay," I say. "Well...bye."

———

New to-do list:

1. Find someplace to put the field hospital's worth of medical supplies I have in various shoeboxes in my room. Too much money and time went into acquiring my latest stash; I'm not dumping it, and I'm not leaving it somewhere it could be taken. So it has to be totally safe, but not in my room.

Wait a minute – Annie and Chase won't be in my room long enough to go through my shoeboxes. I'm being ridiculous. (Unless I leave the room to go to the bathroom...? I will piss myself instead, maybe it will get them to leave sooner.) I'm overthinking it. I'm freaking myself out for no reason. This will be fine. I could just leave the stuff where it is, it's not noticeable to anybody but me. Or I could ask one of my roommates if I could store a few – nope. Nope. They'd hear the pill bottles rattling and open the box right up. I know I would.

I'm looking around my room as though a drop ceiling might have been installed while I wasn't paying attention, or an air conditioning duct, or even a closet, but no – it's an authentic East Williamsburg loft, which means it's a dark, cold former factory that's been carved into too many rooms made of unfinished sheetrock and spackle; basically, when you live there, you get your common areas, and then you get a sheetrock rectangle with a concrete floor. No closet.

This is not usually a problem for me. I own no clothing that requires hanging, except coats, and I have a coat tree for that. My supplies sit in boxes on the floor with several other shoeboxes, in much the same way my books do, and my tubs of files and things, and my suitcase, and everything else I own, except what's in the dresser or on the nightstand. Nobody would think anything of my stash boxes; they blend right in.

And nobody is ever in my room, ever. Except that one time, a few months ago, when Lila followed me home from Collective and confronted me at my door, demanding to see where I lived. After arguing with her on the sidewalk for ten minutes, I agreed to let her come up and see the common space, and to stand at the threshold of my room, but not to enter. "You are really pushing my boundaries," I told her, making us walk up the eight flights of stairs. See if you ever want to come over again after that.

"I'm not here to judge," she said, between gasps. "I want to help."

When we got upstairs, her panting and me not breaking a sweat, I opened the three locks on the door and ushered her in to the apartment. "So...here it is." I showed her the living room, kitchen, etc., and she waved at various roommates and roommate-adjacent people, then we stopped at my door and I unlocked my rectangle, explaining, "I only lock my room when I'm going to be out for the whole day, only because sometimes people have guests and whatever, and they don't know where they're going, and then I have a bunch of Belgians trying to pee in my room."

"Okay." She made the "hurry-up" hand gesture.

"It's kind of depressing," I warned her. "I don't have a window."

"Open it," she said. And when I did, she almost launched forward in surprise. "It's so *clean!*"

"Um." I frowned. "What did you expect?"

"No, I just...." She laughed, relieved. "I was sure you were a hoarder. I thought, 'She's either secretly married to a man, or she's a hoarder, that's why she won't let anybody see her place.' Like, nobody's seen your place! I thought there was some big reason. I seriously thought I was going to open this door and see, like, I don't know what."

I was taken aback. A hoarder? Why would Lila think that? I'm so fastidious; I cleaned her house all the time when I was staying with her. Troubling, that it was so easy for people to believe I was hiding something major in my life. "Like what, wall-to-wall boxes of crap stacked up to the ceiling? Or like jars of pee?"

"No, no." She laughed harder, seeing the look on my face. "No. I'm sorry. I'm so sorry."

I put my hand to my heart, stricken. "I look like a pee collector to you?"

She took two seconds too long to say, "No, no." I gaped at her, aghast, and she laughed so hard she could barely speak. "No...it's not like that, it's just...I'm sorry."

"How is it then? It's a compliment that you think I'm a pee collector? Wait, did you secretly want me to have jars of pee?"

"You're the one who keeps saying 'jars of pee,' not me!"

I slipped off my sneakers and stepped inside. "Well, come on in, then, and let me show you my pee collection. Can you take off your shoes, though?"

She gave me an awestruck look. "Are you seriously...I can come in? You're sure?" She clutched her breastbone like she'd just won an Emmy, and I heard the slot machine go *ching!* in her head. Win! Payout! Gambling is addictive, you know, especially gambling on people.

She spent the next hour sitting on my bed, laughing and apologizing, drinking store-brand flavored seltzer from the bottle and admiring my minimalist decor. I kept teasing her – "You honestly thought I was the Unabomber. You thought I was John Wayne Gacy, there'd be dead little boys in my crawlspace. Oh no, don't apologize! No, that's what I *want* people to think about me!" – and she apologized and laughed some more. "I didn't think that! I just didn't know what to think! I wanted to help, that's a good thing, right?"

The stash boxes throbbed in the corner, but only I saw them.

Lila, her face opened towards me like a lily, was in full flower. She was thrilled that she'd been invited into my room; she hadn't understood why I'd been so uptight about it, and in a way she still didn't understand – why wouldn't I want people to see my immaculately kept room? – but she did understand why I needed to maintain certain boundaries in my life, and she was sorry for barreling past mine. She saw now that she'd been way out of line, and her behavior had bordered on aggressive, even if it was out of love, as she claimed.

"I thought you might need help with something. And I wanted to come and help you. That was my only intention! And in a way, it's good that I'm here, right? That you were able to let me in?" She made a cute forgive-me face. I returned it with a droll oh-please face. "And...after all the time you spent at my place, I wanted to at least see yours."

Good move, reminding me that I owed her, and thus she should be forgiven. "God, I hope I never left any pee jars at your place," I said. "That would be embarrassing."

"One day you have to forgive me."

"I actually think I'm missing a few. Hang on – did you steal my pee jars? I knew it. I knew you were a pee jar thief."

After that night, she reported back to any interested parties that, if anything, I was a neat freak, and that she should have respected my boundaries, and so should everyone else. She'd been to my place, she'd verified it, she'd brought the information back to the group, nobody else needed to go. She was the only person I'd ever let into my room, and she wanted to keep it that way. Nearly a year later, I will still say "pee jar" to her sometimes, because it still makes her laugh.

2. Make sure I'm on the schedule to work all three of those days. Make sure I will still be working there. Do not get fired. DO NOT GET FIRED. Until after Annie and Chase leave, then I think I can get fired. I've seen enough private doctors to do what I needed to do; I can freelance it from here.

3A. Disappear. Start by shutting off my phone. That's a hard one. Shutting off my phone feels like the ultimate in self-punishing behavior. Having a phone in the first place is bad enough. I need to hear it chime all the time, or I'm anxious. I hate that I don't even have to look at it to check my poll numbers; its silence is foisted on me all day and night, with only intermittent relief, and the longer I go without hearing the chime, the worse I feel.

So shutting off the phone should be good for me. The silence is pre-emptive: You're not waiting for a chime because you know it's not coming. I'll un-train myself from the chime-response by going cold turkey, a turkey I will then reheat two days later when I surface again and go back to treating the phone like it's a face-magnet.

It will only be two days, at most.

It'll be good. I don't want to lose my concentration. I need to have a leg up on the rest of the girls; I'll take any leg I can get. Let me be the one who watches and listens, while they're distracted by their cravings and rewards. Let me be the one here in the real world, the one who can look you in the eye with a steady gaze, while everyone else flickers in and out like bad cell reception. Let me pay close attention to you, as you tell me everything I need to know.

I can go phone-free for two days, at least. It will be good for me. Also, it's the only option. I cannot have a phone or even text conversation with any of my friends while Annie and Chase are in town. Having to code-switch abruptly is disorienting, and an unnecessary risk. The 'Lizes must never cross paths, or they will explode.

3B. Dropping social media is not an issue for me. Everyone knows I had to stop using it in high school, because I was being bullied to the point that I nearly killed myself. I do, however, have some very close imaginary friends who are big-time users of social media, so I'm not entirely out of the loop. Through them I can see some of what my friends are posting, sometimes more than I want. It's usually best for me to stay away from that shit entirely, because...it's just better.

4. Hope for the best. Prepare for the worst.

It's been silent on all fronts since the night of Maria's birthday drinks. Normally either Lila or I would have texted the next day to confirm that we loved each other, we were so glad we'd worked things out, and we hoped the other would have a great day, heart heart smile heart smile. But when she didn't text by noon the next day, I realized it was too late for me to text her, because I was already angry that she didn't text me, and then it was weird.

I was also thrown by the idea of Christine reading a text from me over Lila's shoulder, which makes me want to beat her with a length of pipe. I should have got rid of her when she was badmouthing me to Maria; now she's entrenched next to Lila, and she's not going anywhere, and she wants to get rid of me. How did I not see this disaster coming? If I'd known this was in the offing, I'd have offed it right away.

So I wait a day and a half and then write Lila an email:

Liles Liles Chocodiles,
   I have done nothing but think about our talk on Sunday night. Thank you again for being the kick-ass name-taker you are. You really got through to me. I care about you so much, and seeing that I made you unhappy made something crack inside me. I never want to make you cry again (not that I wanted to in the first place).
   I couldn't sleep that night, and I wound up getting out of bed at 3 in the morning and doing what I guess is called an inventory, really looking at the components and systems of my life.
   (Note: I'm sorry this is all about me so far, because this letter is meant to say thank you and to tell you that you are amazing and

beloved. So in case you get bored and stop reading here, that's the important part: you are amazingly beloved.)

But in case you're interested in what you inspired, I found a bunch of resources online, and on Monday I called and made an appointment to see a new shrink on Thursday. And the appointment is at 7:45 a.m. so I can get to work at 9:00 and be on time for work for the first time in my life. I'm terrified by the prospect of talking to a new shrink, especially because of my history with shrinks, but it's time for me to face that fear and at least try, for my friends' sake if not my own.

I know one appointment doesn't mean anything, and I haven't even gone yet, but I already feel more hopeful that I can make positive changes in my life, and when have you ever heard me say that?

Anyway, the first thing you said on Sunday was, I believe, "If you need help, ask for it." You've already helped me more than probably anybody in my life (except Kath), and lately I've felt too ashamed to ask for more. But fuck my stupid ego, you said to ask, so I'm asking for two more things from you:

1. Please don't give up on me. I can't change how I acted in the past, but I'm working to get better. I'd understand if you think I'm so fucked up that you want to walk away from me forever. But I'm asking please, please don't give up on me. You were the only person who believed in me enough to tell me you wanted me to live. I love you, I respect you, and I need you in my life.
2. Please understand if I go dark for a few days. I need to step away from the city and the scene for a little while so I can figure some things out. I've actually been thinking of going to visit my father's grave in Florida, if I can afford it, the next time I have two days off in a row. Can you believe I've never been? But I didn't know him while he was alive, so I always felt like I had no right to go there. Now I think that may be where I need to start this process. (After therapy on Thursday, of course.)

Anyway, if there is any way for *me* to help *you*, I hope you'll ask me. I want to be a good friend to you, too.

Lila, I've said this to you before, many times, but that's because it's been true many times: You saved my life. I am eternally grateful to you. I never want to hurt you again, and if the only way to ensure that is by leaving you alone, that's what I'll have to do. But before I go, I have to at least say these things, because if something happened to me and you didn't know how I felt about you, I'd have to come back as a ghost to tell you, and that would probably freak you out.

I love you, forever, no matter what.

Eliza

PS: You and Christine = fantastic! So happy for you. You deserve all the happiness in the world.

To be clear: The email was *to* Lila, but I wrote it *for* Christine.

I spent perhaps too much time online yesterday, going through Lila's various profiles, where every image, every update, every comment or thumbs-up or smiley or heart was another kick in the gut. And all the while, I'm wondering, *Why am I doing this? Why are you doing this to us, Eliza?* The ratio of pain to satisfaction is too high, it's not worth it, and yet I'm compelled to keep reaching for more. It makes no sense. The lab rat in the experiment who presses a button over and over to get a piece of food, that makes sense. The lab rat pressing a button over and over to get kicked in the balls, that's Facebook.

Every time I clicked on something new, the boot swung into my solar plexus, right in the same spot. And I still kept clicking: click, kick; click, kick; click, kick. Ouch. Ouch. Ouch.

Why? I had to know what I was up against, so I had to spend four consecutive hours getting kicked in the gut, though I probably could have stopped after five minutes. What is there to discover, except that everybody you know is having fun hanging out without you, carrying on these ongoing side conversations with each other, posting things for each other that "reminded me of you," and celebrating each others' birthdays and new jobs and life events you had no idea about and so totally missed? I knew that already, I didn't need to know it anew.

What I didn't know was how long the thing between Lila and Christine had been building until I looked through the last few weeks of Lila's postings and saw the multiple comments Christine left, on subjects ranging from porcupine videos to manipulative relationships: "So cute!" "So true!" "So helpful for me to remember – thank you for posting that! It's like you had me in mind." Wink.

STAB.

I have never acted on a violent impulse, nor would I. I've premeditated on the issue many times, for many hours, but I have gone no further than imagining what I'd do, and then addressing every detail to imagine it even better, then refining the plan and considering the various components for any complications I hadn't yet foreseen, and then thinking about exactly how the violent act would go: what I'd say to them, what I'd want them to say to me, how I would harm them, how I'd get away with it. But that's as far as I've ever gone – thinking about it obsessively for hours over the course of months. Never a step further.

No, there will be no violence. There will be many pushups, burpees, and five mile runs where I'm hurling my feet against the ground because I am picturing running on Christine's face. But there will be no actual, physical, real-world violence. Since I was a child, I've had nightmares where I snap and physically attack someone, and am thrown out of society as a consequence. I won't let that happen in my waking life.

On the picture that served as the happy couple's informal announcement of their intent to be future ex-girlfriends for the rest of their lives – a shot of two wide, white smiling faces side-by-side with the caption, *Very lucky me* – I had my virtual friend Maureen click the thumbs up and say, "Congratulations!!!!!"

My old friend Maureen (sometimes "Mo," to her friends) became online friends with Lila after I introduced them at a bar late one night last year, when Maureen was in town from Atlanta for a few days, which Lila "barely remembers" (probably because it barely happened; I grabbed some drunk girl and asked her to help me make my ex jealous for two seconds in exchange for a whiskey sour). The next day, Maureen added Lila to her friends, and she's been a consistent booster of all things Lila ever since.

The long game, friends. It's like a time travel movie, where you have to go back and plant things in the past that you'll require to help you get back to the future. You must always be planting things, even if you don't know why. One day, you're going to need what they grow.

───────

I am early to work today. When I walk in, my co-workers all stop and look at each other worriedly, like, *It's 9:15 already?*

"Good morning," I say.

And they look at me like, *Good morning?*

I haven't inspired a lot of goodwill around here lately. I've been letting things slide, and I can't do that. But I can't do *everything.* I can't be all the things I signed up to be. I need to let some things go. I have to concentrate – did I say that already? – probably. Bad sign. Remember to concentrate, concentrate on remembering.

In the back room by the lockers, Valencia applies an extra outline of dark purple lip liner before she puts her purse away. Valencia is Goth, something I might have become in my teenaged years if I'd had no other ideas or options. Fortunately, I was able to forge my own very original identity as a bulimic cutter in an institution.

Valencia sees me, checks the clock on the wall, caps her lip liner, and says, "What are you doing here?"

"Good morning," I say, smiling. I decided on the way here that I am going to float through this day, smile and be super-mellow, and have fun making other people miserable by being happier than they are. "New leaf. It's a whole new leaf."

"I thought you were here to talk to Darcy and Raquel. I heard they're going to talk to you."

"Aw, great!" I say. "I bet I'm getting promoted!" I put my hand up for a high five.

She gives me a *what the fuck is wrong with you* look, locks her locker, and leaves.

I am either ignored or given the hairy eyeball from the rest of my co-workers as they come in and out of the locker area. "She's here?" says Raquel from Human Resources, almost walking into me. "Oh! There you are. Wonderful."

"Good morning," I say pleasantly. I don't care about any of this. Whatever the outcome, I'll feel fine; in fact, if they don't fire me, I might quit, because I was ready to slog through this septic tank's worth of shit today, but the idea that I might not have to do it is so appealing, I'm not sure I can resist.

Raquel guides me into the tiny meeting room, then sticks her head back out into the hallway. "Is Darcy out there? Will someone get her and send her in, please?"

I relax in my chair, noticing in my peripheral vision that people keep walking past the open door, trying to get a look at me as I wait for the axe. I breathe deeply and slowly, 1-2-3-4 in, 1-2-3-4 out. A few of these and I feel almost high. I can detach from the scene I'm living in and see it from a distance, like a construction worker atop a building. There's a little guy with an orange vest and a surveyor's tool atop my head right now, his name is Mike, and he's looking around and walkie-talking me what he sees: "Yeah...it looks like Raquel's nervous."

I consider Raquel as she reseats herself at the table. She fires people all the time, why would she be nervous? There must be something unusual here. She's not worried about a discrimination suit, is she? Because everybody in this place is gay: staff, customers, people standing outside waiting for the bus. A lawsuit wouldn't fly, would it?

"Yeah..." says Mike from the roof of my head. "It's not about your orientation. Could be your medical issues, maybe."

Something to keep in mind, as Darcy comes in, closing the door behind her.

Darcy, my manager, has had so much more than enough of me. She's stuffed, she couldn't stand to take another bite, she doesn't ever want to see another me again for the rest of her life. "Eliza," she says, smiling despite herself. "We're here to discuss your termination."

"Okay," I say. I wait for more, but they just look at me. They are applying silence, which is a common negotiation technique.

"Boss?" says Mike. "Sorry to interrupt, but, uh, they don't usually 'discuss' a canning. Usually in these situations, what they do is, they tell you you're fired right away, and then the rest is paperwork. So...I don't know...definitely seems unusual to me."

Raquel says, "Here's the issue: Ordinarily, employees are entitled to a fixed number of paid sick days without a doctor's note, and a limited number of sick days with a doctor's note, that number to be determined on a case-by-case basis."

I nod sagely. That sounds fair. Let's do that, then. Good meeting, everyone.

"So," she says. "We're here to determine your case."

"Okay."

Darcy leans over the table towards me. "Eliza, what are your thoughts about your continued employment here?"

The puzzlement is apparent on my face, I hope. "I think...it would be a good thing...? I'm sorry, I'm not sure what you're asking."

She rephrases it. "Do you feel like you can see yourself continuing to work here?"

"Yes, I do."

Mike's heavy Queens accent comes through, tinny: "Heya, Boss, listen, something's not up to code here, I think they got a problem with the permits." He says perMITS, which I love. He's an excellent surveyor. "This isn't the usual procedure. I wouldn't touch it if I was you."

So I sit tight, meaning, I look blandly at Darcy and Raquel and wait for them to talk. I think of things I could say that would be funny to me but not necessarily to them. They want to make me so uncomfortable that I'll blurt out something like, "I'm not sure I can continue to work here, to be honest," which would screw me very tightly.

Mike called it right away – they don't discuss your firing with you. So there's some reason they feel they can't fire me. So they're trying to get me to dig myself into a hole, and every word I say is another shovelful of dirt. But right about now, they're probably figuring it out: I'm not going to quit, or leave voluntarily, or say anything stupid they could turn into cause for dismissal. So we can all go get waffles or go roller skating or something, because this meeting is over.

But they can't let me back on the floor without some kind of resolution. The rest of the staff would start sicking out all over the place – I would if I was them, which I still am, as of this moment. Darcy and Raquel know that I know that there's something preventing them from firing me; their hand is tipped, and they have none of a kind. So we should all talk about *that*: how funny it is to be in a room with people and share knowledge that you are pretending not to know. I could ask them about HR stuff, the techniques they use to motivate people, the subtle shading of language they have to use that makes sure everything is "true, technically." I love that stuff. I should go into HR. I should take Raquel's job.

"Well," says Darcy. "I'd like to go over the absences and late days, so we can see what we've been working with so far. For instance, last month..."

I lean in to look at the calendar she produces. This should be fun.

On the 15th, I was admitted to the ER with blood loss. I was released on the 16th, I was recuperating on the 17th, I came in to work on the 18th but fainted and was sent home early. The 19th I was recuperating. The 20th I was a half-day late coming from the doctor's. I worked on the 21st. The 22nd I was not on the schedule. The 23rd I worked. The 24th I was two hours late coming from the doctor's. The 25th I had a recurrence of the fainting while on the way to work and had to go to the ER. I had doctor's notes for the appointments and the two ER visits; the two recuperation days were medically necessary and thus excusable.

I was right. That was fun.

The upshot is that nothing happens, and I'm sent out to work the floor, to everyone else's chagrin. The whispers and dirty looks fly as the morning wears on, and by lunch, this girl Jennifer elects herself shop superintendent or something, and comes over to quiz me.

"Hey, Eliza, what happened with Raquel and Darcy this morning?"

"Work stuff," I say cheerfully.

"I know, but, like, did they say anything to you about you not being here, like, all the time?"

I smile. "Why?"

Jennifer has spent the past few hours stewing because I am being treated differently than she is. She has discussed the matter with others, who have confirmed her opinion that yes, this is bullshit, and yes, somebody should say something.

Her voice quickens and rises. "Because you're never here, and the rest of us get stuck working late, and it's like, just because you're anorexic or whatever, doesn't mean the rest of us should have to work harder than you."

Brilliant. Thank you, Jennifer, for speaking to me in a hostile and aggressive manner about my private health matters in such a way as to be overheard by two co-workers and a customer. Sincerely, thank you. Because now the complaint I lodge right away with Raquel puts *you* in danger of being fired, while I am in less danger than ever. Isn't that unfair?

Coincidentally, it's my lunch break.

10

A Mental Splinter

I am given to understand that Christine is sexually very good in bed.

This intel comes from Maria, who I invited to my apartment about twenty-four hours after I sent my email to Lila and received no reply.

I started checking for a reply immediately, then laughed at myself: Give her time to read it, at least, and then absorb it, and then she'll compose a reply. To kill time, I checked in with some of my other selves, combing various online communities for fights I could start or sympathy I could steal. Twenty minutes later, still nothing. I went back to my other selves, then back to no reply from Lila, over and over, for two hours.

Then I took my laptop into the living room and sat with it on one of the couches. It was comforting to hear other people around the apartment, even if we weren't interacting. Sometimes when I sit in my room on my laptop for too many hours at a time, I start to feel like I'm slipping out of this space-time continuum and becoming pure mind, which is a dangerous conceit that mostly leads to me banging the hell out of my forehead or my knee. Being in the living room, where I could see other humans and they could see me, reminded me, *No, this is all real. This is the realm your body lives in, and that makes it real.*

I stayed hunched on the couch for a few hours, peering into

my laptop like it was a Venus flytrap about to snap my head off. People came and went and sometimes said things and I must have replied, and still I doubted the world around me. I didn't feel well. But really, organically unwell, not induced. I felt woozy. I thought about going to an emergency room but I didn't want to move in case I got an email from Lila. The clock on my laptop lost meaning to me long ago; the clock on the kitchen wall was starting to do the same. It couldn't possibly be keeping time. Time doesn't take that long to pass.

I checked and checked and checked my email even though the tab was open on my browser and I could clearly see that no new messages had arrived. But sometimes the new message alert doesn't pop up as soon as the email hits the in-box; sometimes it's as much as five seconds later that it registers, and there you've spent that last five seconds in needless agony. Meanwhile I was arguing with someone in the comments section of a blog post about confronting childhood sexual abuse:

"You know *nothing* about what you're trying to talk about. Penetration is *not* empirically worse than other forms of abuse. You know *nothing* about what it feels like to be asleep in bed and wake up to find your senile grandfather pressing his erection against your back because *he thinks you are your mother*. If you did know, you wouldn't spout such ignorant shit."

Maureen (@MoToMyFriends) was on a roll. Eliza was not. Eliza had not received a response to the unprecedentedly emotional and candid email she'd sent her practically ex-girlfriend seven hours ago. Eliza was in shock. Eliza did not realize she was starting to emit a strange sound, like someone crying very slowly, until Odessa popped her head into the room and said, "Hey, are you moaning? Could you stop?"

By hour twenty, I'd survived a sleepless night spent hyperventilating and seasick from the rolling waves of *this can't be happening, this is happening; this can't be happening, this is happening*. Lila had not replied to my email. Lila was done with me. This was not what was supposed to happen. It was so sudden, so capricious, so unfair. Why wasn't I given some notice, an opportunity to improve myself before my firing?

I got up and went for a two hour run, deliberately leaving the phone at home. When I got home and there was still no reply, I texted Maria with shaking hands:

Hey MayMay, want to have dinner at my house tonight?

Twenty-four seconds later, she replied: YAAASSSSSSS BISH.

But if she's going to continue to talk about Christine's superior sex techniques, I may be forced to ask her to leave.

"She's *really, really* giving," Maria says. "Like, tireless."

Maria and I are sitting on my bed in the corner of my room, propped against the two walls. It's cozy in here, for a concrete and sheetrock rectangle with no windows. There's a cheap carpet remnant on the floor, on top of that is a nicer-looking rug, and a third of the room has two side-by-side workout mats on top of the rug, delineating a neat area for exercise. I put a special adhesive under the mats so they stay fixed in place; if they were sliding around and askew all the time, I would lose my shit. Little things like that are what make me snap.

"I can't fucking believe this," I say for the fiftieth time in a row. Maria looks at me like, *So you mentioned.* I realize that it is bad form to invite a woman over and spend the whole time talking about another woman. "But, doesn't matter. I'm glad you were free tonight, I feel like I haven't seen you alone in a long time."

"You haven't," she says, pointedly. Meaning: No duh, we haven't seen each other alone since our friend-breakup.

"I know. And I miss that...alone time with you. I wish I hadn't been such a jerk."

"You can't help it," she says. "You're just a total selfish asshole."

Wow. A flash of anger – what shit is this, now? Why is everyone ganging up on me? They want me to kill myself. They hate me as much as I hate myself. I hope Maria will feel happy after I kill myself. "I'm sorry," I say. And I've been saying that way too much lately. I hate saying I'm sorry; I only do it when I absolutely must. I said it eighteen times to Lila in my email, and she hasn't even replied. "But I invited you over," I remind Maria. "Kind of a big deal for me."

"Hmmmm," she says, skeptical.

She pokes at one of my socked feet with hers. "Ow," I protest. "Stop kicking."

"Hmmmmmmmmmmm," she says and pokes it again. "You only invited me over to talk about Lila."

"That's not true!" I also wanted to talk about Christine. And to make Lila jealous that I asked Maria over to my place. "I mean, obviously, if your ex is dating my ex, we're going to talk about it. But that's not why..."

She interrupts me. "Lila's not your ex."

"Right, but you know what I mean. Look, we don't even have to..."

And again. "No, I don't know what you mean. I don't think she does either."

"Well..." Now I'm flustered. I thought inviting Maria over would be an opportunity for her to rag on Christine to me, to tell me not to worry about Lila, and hopefully to comfort me while I sob for a while about all the things in my life I can't fix. I'm never going to tell anybody what those unfixable things are, but I can almost bear to think about them when I cry on Maria's lap. "It doesn't matter, because she's my nothing now, and I'm here with you."

Maria leans forward, quite close to me, and puts one hand on my foot. "Am I your ex?"

"What?"

"Do you consider me your ex?"

Jesus Christ, it's a pop quiz. I smile nervously, which is the appropriate answer. "I mean, no...I don't know."

She leans back against the wall and retracts her hand from my foot. "You practically lived with me for three months, you slept next to me four nights a week, we talked and texted and emailed all the time."

"Okay, yeah, and that was great. Being around you...yeah."

Being around her. I remember watching TV and eating cereal with Maria in bed one weekend morning, and how content I was to wash the dishes and spoons and dry them and put them away afterwards, thinking, *I wish this could be my life.* Even though this *was* my life. I saw my dim reflection in the kitchen window, I felt myself breathing, the heft of the dishes was convincing in my hand. This was my life. And yet it wasn't. I got this intensely sad, alienated feeling, and I wanted to go back into the bedroom and tell Maria everything I don't want people to know. But as soon as the idea occurred to me I knew it would be fatal, and I realized that I would never be able to tell anybody who I am. I would never get the chance to be myself in front of another person. I went from elated to suicidal in under a second.

Maria continues. "And then when I asked you to *be* with me, you walked out without a word."

"I know. That was wrong. I'm sorry." Sorry! There it is again!

"Yeah," she says. "That sucked. And then you wouldn't talk to me..."

Oh, come on now. "You wouldn't talk to me!"

"That shouldn't have stopped you from coming up to me like a human person and saying, 'Listen, I don't want us to not talk, so please talk to me.'"

I had no idea Maria was so angry at me, that she has been for months. I wonder if she knew how angry she was before she came over tonight. Maybe she planned for this night to go this way; maybe she got my invitation and thought, "I'm going to take this opportunity to emotionally slaughter Eliza, like I've been dreaming of doing since mid-April." Or maybe, as happens with me too often, she'd planned for the night to go one way, maybe in a romantic direction, and then some feeling came out of nowhere and started using her as its megaphone, and now she can't stop its shouting.

No, that's not it. Her eyebrow is arched and she's smiling coyly. She's having fun. I would be too, if the roles were reversed, and I had all the power. Maybe this *is* what she wanted. I can't tell if she's been denying her anger to herself all this time, or if she was just very skilled at hiding it. I never give anyone credit for being able to hide their emotions; other people are always riddled with tells. They don't know how to control their faces – the secret is to practice, and to have more than one expression on hand, so you don't look frozen. My go-to move, when I'm challenged, is to nod my head as though I'm thinking about it, which allows me to avert my eyes and stall for a second. And you have to learn how to modulate the tone and volume of your voice.

With Maria, though, there's always been something kindred there. We know we're different from the other girls; she alluded to it a few times during our house-playing phase: how we understand emotional exigencies better than most, how we have the balls to do what needs doing. Uberwenches. We've both

taken care of someone we loved as they died of cancer: me with
Kath, Maria with her mother. We don't get to be squeamish or
sentimental about death, like our friends are.

I realize that the whole two hours Maria's been here, I forgot
that I've been waiting for a response from Lila. How funny –
hearing from Lila felt crucial to my survival earlier today; now
I have a new problem. It's both comforting and depressing to
know that Lila can be dimmed in importance, as long as I'm
diverted by something worse. Well, I was hoping Maria would
distract me, and she did.

And now I've had enough of it. I want to stop talking about me
being a shitheel, I want to check my email, I want to go back to
arguing with Lila in my head, I want to put many yards between
me and other humans. I want Maria – my supposed friend, who
I trusted enough to invite over – out of my room, away from my
supplies, away from *me*.

I scooch away from her on the bed. "You know what, I'm
starting to feel kind of not so great, I think..."

She barks a laugh and stays put. "Ha! What a surprise. You
conveniently feel sick when I'm trying to have this conversation
with you."

Conveniently sick? What's that supposed to mean? Whatever
my authentic nervous face is, I'm sure she's seeing it right now.
"I've been sick for the past six months," I say, self-righteous.
"There's nothing convenient about it."

"Oh, I know. Don't worry, everybody's well aware that you've
been sick. That's why nobody wants to upset you, so they let you
get away with your shit."

I feel my eyes bulging, ready to jump out of my face to save
themselves from what's coming. Nothing's coming, idiot, says
the voice of reason. And nobody can prove anything, because
there's nothing to prove. Stay haughty, Eliza. Remember, you
are the one being wronged. "What do you mean, 'everyone
knows?' What am I 'getting away with?'"

"Nothing," says Maria. "Calm down. I'm just saying, you felt
fine ten minutes ago, before I brought up the issue of you and
me. The issue of *you*, really. I have no issues." She makes a kiss-
face and pretends to fluff her hair to emphasize her superiority.

Calm down, calm down. Everybody knows you're full of shit,

but calm down. My voice breaks. "What do you want me to say? I said I'm sorry. I said you're right, okay? There, I just said it again. I feel like nothing I say is going to make a difference to you, and my stomach genuinely hurts, and yeah, this conversation is painful. The thing with Lila is painful. I poured my heart out to her, I told her over and over I'm sorry, I'm sorry, and now she won't even speak to me." I break down and cry, one hand shielding my eyes. "I can't deal with this right now. I really can't. Please. I don't feel well, and I know you think I'm faking it, but it's real, and it hurts right now..."

Is she going for it? Her arms are folded, she's not saying anything, and I can't see her face. No, she has no sympathy for me. I can't cry myself out of this one. This thought unlocks another, deeper level of grief in me, and I sink down into the subbasement of despair.

Here are the skeletons of dead and buried hopes: The hope for a mother to tell me she loves me. The hope for a father of any kind. The hope for any other living person to be related to by blood besides Annie. The hope that this craving that drives me could be satisfied someday. The hope that I could stop hiding from everyone I've ever known in the past. The hope for a friend who would love me as much when I'm healthy as when she thinks I am near death. The hope that this story ends in any other way besides my suicide. The hope for something to hope for. This one still has some flesh on it. I just buried it last week.

"Shhhhhh," says Maria, softer now. She crawls over to drape her arms around me. "Okay, it's okay."

And now I'm exactly where I wanted to be, sobbing in Maria's arms. But I'm sobbing because she's onto me, she hates me, and now everything is ruined for me here, and it's either kill myself or start over again, and I can't start over again. It takes so much out of me. I'm so tired of all of it. I wish I could change. If there were a rehab for people like me, I'd go there, but I've gone to plenty of places, and there's never been anybody who can help me. I feel so fucking sorry for myself. I'm so sad that I have to live such a lonely life. I keep crying and crying. Maria adjusts her arm to make it more comfortable for me.

"Shhhhhh," she says. "It's okay."

I shake my head no and sob some more. It's not okay.

Everybody hates me. Everybody at work hates me, every one of my friends hates me, and they don't even know the half of it. Think how much more they'd hate me if they knew who I was. Think how much I hate myself. It comes to me again – the very clear feeling that I should throw myself on the mercy of Maria and confess while she holds me like a pieta. I don't even know what I'd say.

Maria, I'm a liar. Every story I've ever told you about my past is a lie, everything I say in the present is a lie, and unless some kind of miracle happens, I'm going to be lying for the rest of my life. When things get too bad for me, I make myself sick – I take someone else's medication, or otherwise ingest something I shouldn't – because it's the only way I know how to make people care about me. Everything I do is calculated to make someone else feel or think or do something. I haven't had a genuine friend since I was eight years old. I'm afraid I'm going to take the wrong thing and die, not because I want to kill myself, but because this thing wants to kill me.

"Hey," says Maria, releasing me from her arms and studying my fucked-up face. "It's okay. I'm sorry I was mad. I didn't mean to come over and get in a fight with you. I just care about you. Everyone cares about you. And we see you sick, and we see you struggling, and it's frustrating, because you refuse to take care of yourself. It's like, if there's something you should do to get better, you do the opposite."

I nod, trying to pull myself together, but this slays me. She has no idea how right she is. The day I cut myself at work after taking the Warfarin and it wouldn't stop bleeding, I thought, *Is this it? Am I dying today? But wait, it's only supposed to happen on my terms.* I feel like I'm going to pass out just thinking about it, losing all that blood, trying to staunch the wound, knowing I was about to faint and would no longer be able to help myself. Two and a half pints is all you can safely lose, said the internet, for someone my size; more than that, and you could easily die.

Maria frowns. "Jesus, you really don't look good. Here, lay back, okay? Do you need to throw up?" She looks around for my wastebasket and my panic spikes. *Don't touch anything.*

I am pale, clammy, trembling. I don't know the last time I

threw up when it wasn't my own doing. "I'm okay," I say, lying back on the bed as her hands guide me. "I'll be okay."

"I'm getting you some water," she says. "I'll be right back. Yell if you need to puke."

I lie on my back and try to slow my heart rate. I'm okay, nothing is really wrong with me. It's the workout. I'm dehydrated. Plus the stress. The pills are weakening my heart...no, they're not. You're just freaked out. My pulse marches through my body, like it did when I was a girl of five, and I put my ear against my inner wrist to hear the steady trump trump trump trump like the sound of boots on the ground, the army of my blood.

I was that little girl once. Nobody ever saw her then, and nobody will ever see her again. I try to reach out to her and tell her she's not alone, but she can't hear me, because she *is* alone. This strikes me as the saddest thing I have ever known.

Maria comes back with water. "Don't sit up. Here." She slides the pillows under my head. "Can you drink this, or will it make you puke?" I take the glass, take a sip. It's painfully refreshing. Sometimes I run and I don't drink any water afterwards, I don't know why. Oh, wait – to hurt myself, that's why.

She takes the glass and puts it on my nightstand. Then she gets back onto the bed and lies down next to me, propped up on one shoulder, looking intently at my face. She is so present, so aware of everything going on in this moment, in this bed. What does she know? What does she want to know?

She reaches out and puts her hand against my wet cheek. I like to sleep that way, curled on my side with my hand under my cheek. I can't really sleep without it. There has never been a single bit of comfort from anywhere outside myself. Maria – I wish I could explain. If I was ever going to tell anybody, it'd be you.

"I love you," I say. Not to disarm her, not to flatter her, not to hear it back from her, but because it's true.

"I love you too," says Maria. She sighs. "I do. I know you're fucked up, but I don't care, so's everybody else, and you're more interesting. I love you, and I want to be your friend."

That's how I wind up inviting her to meet my mom.

———

The email from Lila comes three days after I sent mine, and by that point, I already know what she's going to say. You don't delay a reply that says *that's great, I love you too*; those you send right away. The not-so-good emails take longer to draft.

> Dear Eliza,
> I needed a few days to think how I wanted to reply to your email because our relationship is one that is important to me. I am glad to hear you recognize the many ways in which you have been hurtful to me and that you are making a plan for yourself that includes therapy.

[Okay, "One that is important to me?" "In which you have been hurtful to me?" Read this to yourself in robot voice; it sounds perfectly natural.]

> "I'm sorry this is all about me," you said. That's the only time you used the words "I'm sorry." You didn't apologize to me for the ways in which you have been hurtful to me recently. You know your irresponsibility has caused me a lot of unhappiness and I deserve a real apology. But I don't expect one.

[Ooh! Burn.]

> I'm not giving up on you but I am giving up the unhealthy relationship we have formed. I care about you but enough is enough.
> Lila

[Christine. Or, a combination of Christine and some TV shrink's book about "the healing journey," or whatnot.]

It's amazing how much has changed in the five days since I hugged Lila outside the bar, but what's more amazing is that things were ever the way they were before this week. It feels natural that Lila and I will have no contact for a while – we were sick of each other, but we couldn't see it. Now we can see nothing but. Her martyr act was just as grating as my victim act. It's not like I'm the first person who ever sponged off somebody and then didn't date them; it's not like I'll be the last person in her life to take her for granted. If her relationship with me is the worst thing that ever happens to her, she'll be very lucky.

There's still an ache in me, because she was a big part of my mental life, and now she can't be. Fortunately, my murderous hatred of Christine has been keeping me busy. Preparing for my mother's visit has been time-consuming, too; plus, I've been hanging out and texting with Maria a lot. I feel closer to her after the night in my room, almost like I did confess, and she did forgive me, even though no such thing happened.

I'm nervous about introducing her to Annie and Chase. But Chase likes to talk a lot; I'll ask him what he thinks of New York, and how he thinks New York City differs from central Florida, and he'll talk from the minute the breadbasket hits the table all the way to the bill. If the conversation begins to wander into uncomfortable territory, I'll ask another question: *How is the convention going? What do you think of the hotel room? Mom, what'd you think of the September 11 museum? I know, all those poor people.* We'll stay off the topic of the nature of my relationship with Maria, and we'll avoid talking about any part of my past.

"I can't believe I get to meet your mom," Maria gloats. She's sitting on my bed, birthplace of this foolhardy idea. This is only her second visit, but she's already made herself comfortable in my room. Earlier, she was starting to poke around near my boxes and files until I gave her a pointed look.

"I know," I say. "I can't believe it either."

"I didn't even know you were in touch with her."

I already scanned my mental archives, but I scan again: What exactly have I told Maria about my mom? Just the usual stories. Nothing anyone would bring up at a dinner table.

"I wasn't, for a while. I didn't talk to her for two years when I was drinking and fucked up. Then I only talked to her to get her to help me. We're on better terms now – still not great, but...I don't know. We're both trying. I haven't seen her since I got to the city, and since they were already going to be in town for Chase's thing..."

"I'd understand if you never wanted to talk to her again."

She reaches up and makes a grasping motion, which means, *Come here and sit with me.* I obey. It's a whole new relationship since our "breakthrough" night, and she is optimistic about the future. The fact that I invited her over, opened up to her, and am now holding her hand in public when she wants me to are all significant signs of progress in the right direction. Now I am introducing her to my mother. It's clear that I'm on my own healing journey; it is inevitable, she reasons, that one day I will be healed and journeyed enough to have a real relationship with her.

Girls love it when you improve under their care. Maria feels proprietary over me, now that she knows for sure that nobody understands me the way she does. She's going to fix me, she will succeed where no other has prevailed, and that will prove her superiority, not only to Lila, but to everybody else I ever met. And she deserves that credit. I want to give it to her. I want everybody to know that Maria is fixing me.

I especially want Christine to know that Maria is fixing me, and I hope she burns with the acid of a thousand refluxes when she considers the two of us together. This isn't even about Lila anymore. It's about me and Christine. I've been trying to figure out, aside from the wonderful sex she does, what her appeal might be, this dowdy, loud, moralizing rhino – that's how I see her, like a rhino from a children's book, an upright rhino in pearl earrings and an ill-fitting dress.

So far what I've gleaned from Maria is that Christine is a control freak who takes care of everything ("Oh yeah, Christine totally wrote this," Maria said, when I showed her Lila's reply to my email), and this caretaking can be very attractive, especially to people who usually do all the caretaking themselves. So she's a mommy figure with a car – and the car is important, because the car has the potential to take you someplace fun, while you sit in the shotgun seat with your feet on the dash singing the wrong words to the song on the radio. Everybody loves singing in the car.

Eventually, though, you start to feel weird about fucking someone who acts like your mom, and she becomes an overbearing pain in the ass, and *you* want to run your *own* life for a change, and you wind up being attracted to trouble like me.

"So what should I know about your mom and...what's his name? Chuck, Chip, Chase? Like, is there stuff I shouldn't say?"

"Don't tell them I'm gay," I say. "They haven't figured it out."

"*You* haven't figured it out."

"I mean, say whatever you want, I don't know. You don't have to tell her I got fired from the Collective – she knows I 'moved on,' or whatever, but I didn't tell her, 'Oh, I got canned.'"

Maria nods. She gets it. I've been in the room when her father's called, and she unconsciously adopts a higher voice and a sunnier personality because she doesn't want him to worry about her. You never want to let your parents know you're not doing well; you don't want to disappoint them, because then you'll resent them for being disappointed in you. It's just better to edit the narrative of your life when you're talking to your parents. Everyone knows that.

I continue in this vein. "I don't tell her every little thing about my health, because I don't want her to worry and make everything worse."

She nods. "I mean, she knows you were in the hospital in May, right?"

"Oh yeah, she knows. We don't have to talk about it if it doesn't come up, though."

In fact, here's a list of subjects let's avoid:

My father
My grandfather
My childhood
My childhood molestation
My suicide attempts
My institutionalization
My hospitalization
My health
My mental health
Kath's death
Pretty much anything else I've ever talked about with respect to my past

"Can I tell her you're a big slut?" asks Maria. "Can I tell her we're getting married and buying some sperm and you're going to carry my sperm-baby?"

"Or, you know what, we could just call the whole thing off and sit around here, and you could watch me get in an argument with my hairbrush about the phrase 'God as you understand him,' and whether or not twelve-step is inherently sexist."

"I won't mention our satanic rituals, then."

Look at us. We're a couple, making jokes, working off each other's material, teasing each other. From the outside it looks real. This is what's really happening. Is Maria feeling it too? Is she standing back and observing herself, composing each face and gesture and then marveling at how natural it all looks, as though it's really happening? To what end?

I'm staring, trying to read her mind, trying not to let her read mine. She says, "Take a picture, it'll last longer."

I wish this was my life. This is my life. Every moment of comfort costs me a moment of fear. The more I love, the more I suffer. I think ahead to when this will all fall apart, and I want to die.

11

Hard Facts

This is untenable, I say to the Maureen in my head.

The Maureen in my head knows. She's watched me suffer all week, as my mom's visit impends and Lila continues to be silent. I'm afraid, which I rarely am – I don't tend to get afraid unless it's warranted, so when I do feel afraid, I know things are truly bad, and that makes me more afraid. It's a Versailles effect of fear.

I can't... I say, fumbling for the rest, then I realize that's a complete sentence. I can't.

Well, we have to, says Maureen. Death is not an option.

No? But death would solve so many problems. Just think of the funeral, everybody weeping and blaming themselves...

We don't have time for the funeral fantasy right now. We have to focus on reality.

I smack myself in the face. The sting is supposed to remind me that this is what's real: the hand, the cheek, the blood vessels and the nerves. I am in my room, today is Tuesday afternoon, I didn't show up for work this morning, even though I "meant to," and since I "meant to," doesn't that cover it? I pictured it, I can picture it now...my fingernails are too long...

Another slap.

Eliza! This is important. Pay attention. We have a number of things to go over. Number one: You can't tell Maria the truth. You can not, and you must stop thinking about it, because right now you're so afraid you're going to do it, it makes you want to do it just to get it over with. Do you understand me?

I do. I do understand the me that is Mo, and I'm grateful she decided to step up and take over, because this is the kind of solid, real-world advice I need. I've been waffling lately, not knowing how to be, but she is reminding me. Be hard, be ruthless, be right.

Annie is coming tomorrow, and I have taken to carrying a variety of pills on my person, so in case of emergency, I can break glass. Or a bone. Whatever it takes to get me out of the action. I know this is a last resort, because if I am hospitalized while my mom is in town, there will be way too many people talking candidly to each other without my interpolation. I know this. I'm simply carrying the pills as a kind of security blanket. Which, if necessary, I can fashion into a parachute.

This is the kind of muddled thinking that Maureen is here to address.

Eliza, put the pills away. You're not getting hospitalized while your mother is in town. You're not going to faint, vomit, or bleed for the entire two days of her visit, nor will you do so in the two days leading up to it. This is going to be an uneventful 96 hours, and when you're on the other side of it, you're going to be very glad you maintained instead of crumbling.

I want to agree with myself. I *do* agree with myself. I'm right – I can do this, and I can do it the smart way. Dinner will be nerve-racking, but the things I'm most worried about surfacing are not things that people talk about at the dinner table. Maria specifically asked me if there are things she shouldn't say in front of Annie and Chase, so I know she'll be discreet. Whatever happens, I've talked my way out of worse before.

I can get through dinner. I can get through the whole visit. I can wear the Eliza suit and the Eliza mask and the Eliza wig. I can have the Eliza backstory. I can be her for 96 hours, no problem. It's the rest of my life I'm worried about.

———

Tuesday, 6:48 p.m.

Hey Lila, it's Eliza's friend Maureen. Sorry to bother you but I am really worried about Eliza. I can't get in touch with her, I thought maybe you might know what's up. I know getting the diagnosis was hard for her. You're the person she always talks about most so I thought you might know where she is. If you hear anything and you can let me know she's okay I would be very relieved. If I hear anything I will let you know too. Thanks. Sorry again for the weird email. I'm just worried.

As the evening hours pass with no reply to Maureen's message, I picture Lila and Christine at Lila's house. It's messy, of course, because I'm not around – when I was there, the place was meticulously cleaned – but Christine tolerates the mess for some reason, maybe because it makes Lila seem like the younger and flakier of the two of them, and they both need a visual reminder that Lila is the lesser in their relationship. I assume they spend most of their time at Christine's anyway, but I've never been there, so I have to set it at Lila's.

Lila is on her laptop on the couch. She is wearing more than one pair of socks, as ever. There are stockings that go up to her thigh, then tube socks that go up to her calf, then some little footie socks in a coordinating color. She's taken out her hairband and wears it on her wrist, a little tangle of hair caught in one spot, and it's that tangle – so unstudied and intimate – that just kills me, as she moves her fingertips over the trackpad, scrolling through Maureen's note.

Christine's next to her on her laptop, and music is on in the background. Lila rereads the note. She would like to respond to Maureen, but Christine is right there, and even though Christine's absorbed in her own flytrap, she could get up to go to the bathroom at any moment, and nothing is more suspicious than someone clicking off a page the second you stir from your seat. Also, how would Lila respond? She has no idea how I am. She doesn't even know what "the diagnosis" is supposed to refer to, but it sounds bad.

She is flattered, though, to be the one I talk about the most with Maureen. Rumors of my handholding with Maria must have reached her – they better have reached her – and hearing about it made Lila feel too easily replaced. The brief spark of satisfaction from this flattery ignites her self-hatred – how stupid must she be, to still give a shit about her place in my life? I used her, I am a classic manipulator, I am a psychic vampire. Lila has no place in my life, nor do I have one in hers. Christine is adamant about this.

But I may be in trouble. What if I'm killing myself right now? Lila hasn't spoken to me in two weeks – how's she going to feel if I die, knowing she had the chance to stop my suicide and she didn't?

Maybe if she hadn't cut me off, I wouldn't be disappearing like this. Now she resents Christine. Christine's the one who made her cut it off so definitively; Lila felt good about our friendship after our talk outside the bar. She thought we might be able to work things out. God, that was only two weeks ago.

At home, I am my own voodoo doll. People like to say they're "waiting on pins and needles," but they have no idea what that really feels like, unless they're pricking themselves in the hip with a sewing needle that's been blackened with a match, like I am. Feel my pain, Lila. Think about me. I am thinking about you so hard it seems impossible that you could think about anything else but me. Especially with the note from Maureen open on your lap, especially knowing how desperate I am...

Lila thinks about texting Maria to see if she's heard from me, but that would make her feel pathetic; also, Christine would ask her, *Who are you texting?* Christine always announces who she's texting, because she assumes that Lila is interested in every single interaction she has during the course of a day, and that Lila wants to reciprocate by sharing her own. So far, this has been no problem.

Lila thinks she'll write back to Maureen and give her Maria's number, let them sort it out. That's the right idea. It's probably a false alarm, but in case it isn't, at least she'll have done something instead of nothing. She wouldn't be able to live with herself if something happened and she'd done nothing.

She goes for her phone to look up Maria's number, and the rhino rears its predictable head.

"Who are you texting?"

She's not going to tell Christine, because she doesn't want to spend the next two hours listening to Christine scold her for being worried about me when this is obviously another manipulative false alarm. In truth, Lila's a little tired of hearing about what an asshole I am. She doesn't like Christine implying that she made a mistake loving me, or that she has bad taste in people.

"Nobody," says Lila, thwarted. "Just double-checking the date. Can you believe it's the 31st already?"

Now she's a liar, just like me. She closes the window with Maureen's note, looks over the lid of the laptop, and smiles at Christine, as their relationship flips like an hourglass and starts pouring out its sand.

———

Wednesday, 8:31 a.m.

Hey Lila, I wanted to let you know I heard from Eliza around 4 a.m. last night and she sounded really fucked up. I hate to say this but I think she was drinking and that scares me. If she goes off the wagon now, I don't know what's going to happen.

I told her I reached out to you and she's not speaking to me now, because she says you don't care about her and I shouldn't have contacted you. She'd kill me if she knew I was writing to you again but I wanted to let you know that she's alive. If you hear from her, could you please let me know? Thanks.

I should have stayed at Maria's last night. I wanted to be alone because I thought Lila would reply to Maureen and maybe the two of them could have a nice lengthy back-and-forth, but since that didn't happen – since Lila probably didn't even blink before deleting the note; she was probably at Christine's when it came through, having a sixty-nine – I spent the night writhing in the all-too-familiar agony of losing someone's love.

How could Lila say she loved me two weeks ago, and not even care if I'm alive or dead today? How could she turn her back on me like this? She stopped loving me. She did love me, but now she doesn't, because that's how awful I am.

I can't.

I begin suiting up for a beast of a workout, a brutal endurance session to remind myself what I can endure. I am also thinking about taking one more Warfarin from Odessa's bottle, even though I am not planning to take the one I already have, no siree ma'am, so I really don't need another. Except I don't care what I need; I want it, and I'm going to take it. Not *take it* take it; not ingest it. Just take it to have.

My mom is coming to town tonight, and Lila is abandoning me. I deserve some kind of special treat. I award myself possession of one more Warfarin.

The roommates with day jobs are getting ready for work. We have a schedule for the shower-bathroom, and though I missed my official 7:40 to 8:00 window, our 8:40 to 9 roommate, Jess, is away somewhere this week, so I know I can slip in behind Bernard as he exits and there's a good twenty minutes before Odessa needs to get in there.

But Bernard is running behind today, or his girlfriend is in there, because I have to wait ten minutes more than I should. I spend the time seething outside the door, pacing and muttering. I want to go out and run now, *right* now, and every second of delay infuriates me exponentially. How inconsiderate can people be? I am in physical pain right now, and they are preventing my relief.

Finally Bernard's girlfriend exits, simpering at me, and I enter, slamming the door shut. I just want to get what needs getting and get out of there. I don't even look at myself in the mirror – now is not the time for that – before I'm in the medicine cabinet, prying the lid off Odessa's prescription bottle, trying to shake one out into my palm without spilling all of them, going to replace the bottle. Which is when Odessa walks in, be-robed, for her shower.

We're both startled. She must have decided to shower early in Jess' absence, but why am I in there? I'm obviously not showering now, since it's clear that I'm pre-workout, and if I had to excrete, I'd use the toilet-bathroom. With no pocket handy, I toss the pill into my mouth and replace the bottle, rummaging around in the cabinet. "Hey, have you seen my Aleve?"

Odessa butts me out of the way of the sink, frowning into the medicine chest. "What are you doing?"

I'm trapped between her and the toilet. I put my hands up. "I'm looking for my Aleve, I thought it was in the kitchen, but then..."

Odessa is having none of this. She is not a wishy-washy person, she doesn't care about offending me, and she is not afraid she might be mistaken. She knows what she saw. "Why are you in my medicine?"

"I'm not in your medicine!" I say. "Why would I be in your medicine?"

"I don't know," she says, staring me down. "But that's my bottle you had in your hand." She yanks her pill bottle out of the cabinet and tucks it into the pocket of her robe. "I'm counting my pills, and I better not be missing any, because I had to go to the drugstore two days early last month. I knew I was running out of them too soon."

"Count your pills, I don't care! Why would I steal your medication? I didn't steal your medication! Whatever." I push past her and go to my room, where I lock my door from the inside.

Okay, this is bad. This is abysmally bad. This day started out awfully, and it is only getting worse. Odessa caught me, and it's not going to take her very long to realize the link between her medication and my health issues, and then she is going to tell everyone, and I will have to find another apartment. That won't be the end of it, either; New York is too small a town for me to disappear in. I'm going to have to go away and start over again.

I want to leave the house right now. I want to go for my run, because as long as I'm running, I'm not dealing with this problem, but then I realize I can't run, because I swallowed the stupid pill, and now I have to be afraid of the smallest scrape. Also, now I have to get rid of my stash as soon as possible – well, I'll keep a few of the pills, but I'll have to dump the majority of them, along with the syringes, the tourniquet, the sling, the roll of gauze padding, the razor blades. The whole shoebox, with drops of my blood on the underside of the lid.

Annie is coming tonight. She and Chase will be checking in to their hotel around six-ish, then they want to come over and see my place. Dinner with Maria is tomorrow; the day after that, they're gone. I can't fathom the paradise my life will be when all this is over.

I put the shoebox in a duffel bag, grab my wallet and phone, throw on a sweatshirt and jeans, and put my ear to the door so

I can hear if Odessa's in the hall. It's quiet, except for the sound of the shower running, so I decide to make a break for it, and I'm out the front door of the apartment in seconds. I didn't lock the door to my room, but that's okay – anything I was afraid of people finding in there is gone. Let Odessa search through my room while I'm out today. I've got nothing to hide.

———

Today would be a great day to go to work. It's raining and chilly outside, I have nowhere to go, and nothing to think about except how fucked I am. I briefly consider going in to the store, explaining that I was unwell yesterday, and putting on the t-shirt that makes me one of many interchangeable SALES PALS who will be happy to HAPPY TO HELP YOU, instead of the uniquely recognizable ELIZA MADIGAN from the Wanted posters all over town. What a joy and relief it would be to greet people from behind a register, scan gun in hand, and ask each one with hearty concern, "Did you find everything you were looking for today?" But there's no safe haven to be found there anymore; another respite I ruined.

I take the subway into midtown and walk to the library on Forty-First Street – not the big famous one, but the smaller branch across the street, where there are computers you can use when you don't want your activity to be traceable back to you. I don't need to go online right now; I'm just here for the sanctuary, because this is a place I've come in the past when I needed to cover some tracks. I get as comfortable as I can in one of the armless wooden chairs and try to think.

- Annie and Chase will be here in a few hours. I can't take them to my apartment, as I promised I would, in case Odessa is there running her mouth. I don't know how I'm going to explain this to them.

- I don't know what's going to happen when I eventually go back home. No doubt, Odessa will have told the other roommates she saw me stealing her pills, and they're going to kick me out. I'll have to find a new place without a reference

from my current roommates, and stories will spread about
the crazy girl who stole her roommate's medication, until
someone recognizes me in the description and says, "Eliza
Madigan? I know her." And then I'm done in New York.

- Lila still hasn't replied to Maureen to see if I'm okay.

Why does this one feel like the worst problem out of all
of them? When I think about Lila abandoning me, I want to
go full-on lupine, to howl like a wolf and shred my skin with
my claws and bite people to death. But I can't let myself be
distracted by Lila right now. I have to concentrate on figuring
out a plan. I have to make a plan to keep Annie and Chase
squared away, and a plan to deal with the situation at the
apartment.

And a plan to get Lila to love me again.

I can't help it – this is the one I seize upon, or the one that
seizes upon me, the one that chomps down on me like a tiger
mauling a magician.

- First I have to get rid of Christine. Christine's the one who's
  keeping us apart.

- But Christine's not going anywhere unless she wants to go. I
  have to make her want to break up with Lila.

- Why would Christine want to break up with Lila?

- Because Christine finds out Lila is still in love with me.

- She's not, which is the whole reason behind this tedious
  exercise.

- But I could make it look like she is.

Yes. Oh, thank God – after two weeks of suffering Lila's silence,
finally, an answer to the problem. Why didn't I think of it
before? I will anonymously supply Christine with proof that
Lila is in love with me, and that she has lied to Christine about
her whereabouts in order to spend time with me. Christine will
totally buy it, Lila won't be able to refute it, and it will be *au
revoir* Christine.

I feel myself coming back to life – the real me, Eliza, whose prodigious intelligence and powers of imagination have allowed her to survive lo these twenty-four years, not the twit who cowers under the bed.

- The Odessa thing is a problem, but nothing she says can be proved. I can go home and declare my intent to move out because I'm so indignant over what she's accused me of.
- Annie and Chase? I'll think of something, I always do, and no matter what transpires at dinner with Maria, I'll handle that too.

My courage is replenishing, my faith in myself is being restored. I've been going missing lately, but I'm back now, and boy, am I grateful to see me. I am the one person who can get me out of this sea of shit; I am the helicopter and the pilot and the dangling ladder, and I can hear the *thuk-thuk* sound of me swooping in to save the day

There's just one loose thread that's nagging me, and that's Maria. I haven't heard from her since yesterday afternoon. That's not been our style, we've been fairly texty lately. I pick up my phone and tap out a short *What's up, Gorgonzola?* – a reference to a conversation from last week. She was hating on her own appearance and she called herself a Gorgon; I said, "More like a Gorgeous." She enjoyed that one.

Maria. I pine for her. I can't wait to read her response, to find out what silly random thing my text inspires in her. I feel better just thinking about her. Look, things are back to normal now! Maybe I will go online, start looking for a new apartment, check to see if Maureen finally got a response from Lila.

I go for my phone again. Note that Maria hasn't texted me back right away. Again, this could be circumstantial; perhaps some person is demanding her attention. Maybe there is a meeting. She does graphic design at a marketing firm, and most of her day is spent by herself with headphones on, phone right next to her on her desk, but maybe she is in the bathroom. No, she takes her phone there too.

It would be nice to hear from Maria sooner rather than later. I texted her yesterday and she didn't hit me back, and now today... Is she having second thoughts about meeting my mom? Has she heard from Lila? If so, she should be calling to make sure I'm all right. Unless their conversation went a different way.

I check Maureen's messages. Lila hasn't replied to her. The sight of Maureen's two messages sitting there − one atop the other, no reply in between or after and none to come; those poor, pathetic, neglected messages just wanting to be answered, the way any message wants − is so upsetting, I have to cringe and squeeze my eyes shut as Maureen types:

> Wednesday, 3:07 p.m.
> So I guess Eliza was right, you don't care about her. I thought you were a different kind of person so thanks for proving me wrong. When she kills herself I hope you know it's your fault.

I hit send before I go on for pages, telling Lila what a hypocrite she is, cataloguing every lie she told me over the past two years, reminding her that I forgave her for getting me fired, and she should forgive me for...I don't even know what she's angry at me about! What did I do? She won't even tell me what I did that's making her not speak to me! It's so unfair!

She's killing me. Lila wants me to die. Lila wants me to kill myself. She is never speaking to me again, that much is clear. I might as well be dead in her mind. I will never know how she could abandon me overnight, I will never understand, and it will plague me for the rest of my life, which won't be long now, because the only way I can win this fight is to commit suicide, blame it on her, and ruin the rest of her life, all of it, every slow, ugly second of it.

And Maria's not texting me either. What the fuck?

I felt so clear and confident a minute ago, before I saw Lila's lack of response. Now I'm back to feeling like this is the worst and quite possibly last day of my life. By now, that's a comforting thought, because one way or another this day's going to end.

Then my mom calls.

I put her call through to voice mail and leave the library to return it, because only monsters and war criminals talk on their phones in the library. She and Chase have just landed at Newark

Airport, and will be making their way into the city during rush hour. "Great!" I say, though I'd been praying for their plane to crash. "Can't wait to see you!"

I have a minimum of an hour and a maximum of two hours before they will be at the hotel, where I am meeting them...to do what with, I don't know.

- I can't bring them home to my apartment tonight.
- I may not be able to bring Maria to dinner with them tomorrow night.

This looks bad. This is bad-looking, for sure. I can't deliver anything I promised. So what can I give them instead? What is it that they really want from me?

My mother wants an intimate experience of what it's like to be me. She wants to see the backdrops of my daily life, so she can move the paper doll in my likeness against realistic scenery in her head. She wants more accuracy and authentic detail in her vicarious living of my life. It will make her feel closer to me, if she is able to imagine me more clearly. I have to give her some piece of the Eliza Madigan Experience.

I can't bring her home. I can't bring her to somebody else's home. I can't bring her to work. I could bring them to the ramen place, but that's not going to fly.

Ah ha. I can bring them to the Collective – I think there's a poetry reading tonight, which would make this the most welcome poetry reading of my life. They'll get to see the place I worked, a real-life lesbian bookstore-café with authentic might-as-well-be-purple people; they'll whisper hello and smile at whoever is behind the counter, and then we'll GTFO and get some Indian food.

Worst case, Lila's there, but who cares if Lila sees me looking perfectly sober and cool when I'm supposed to be hurling myself off the wagon and slashing my wrists for love of her? Fuck her. My friend Maureen told me she reached out to Lila on my behalf, and though it pissed me off that Maureen did that, it pisses me off more that Lila didn't even acknowledge the messages. That's just rude.

Still, it might not have been the best idea to have Maureen send that last message. I just blew ten months of being Maureen in three lines of text, and now that alias is burnt. She can't be Facebook friends with Lila now; I'll have no way to view Lila's profile, and though that will wind up being a good thing, right now it feels like I've been guillotined. I'm a severed head in a basket, trying to figure out where the rest of me went.

The rain has let up as I walk over to Times Square. I have some time to kill before I meet Annie and Chase at the hotel, so I sit on the wet steps at Duffy Square, looking at my phone. Nothing from Maria, nothing from Lila, nothing from anybody who matters at all. But that's okay. With the Warfarin in me, all I need is one good swipe at my arm with the razor in my left front pocket, and they'll live the rest of their lives regretting how they treated me.

Speaking of my razor, I need to get rid of the shoebox. I meant to leave it at the library, but I forgot, maybe because I don't actually want to get rid of it. Haven't I given up enough recently? Maybe I'll just hang on to it for a little bit. I can always ditch it somewhere, maybe the ladies' room at the hotel, or wherever we go to eat.

I am dreading this night and have been for weeks, but when I enter the lobby of their hotel and my mother comes towards me, I'm struck by how glad I am to see her. Maybe it's because I don't have anybody else in the world, but I realize that I miss her. I always have. At forty-eight, she is still a beautiful woman; the lines and the little jowls don't entirely ruin her face, especially when she is smiling, as she is now.

"Hi Honey."

"Hi Mom."

She actually hugs me, which is rare; usually I get some awkward air-hug, like she's appalled by the idea of her body touching mine, but this time she embraces me before she lets go. She is still petite, perhaps a few inches broader at the hips than she was when I was a kid, but no more. I see her register how thin I am, the ropy muscles I cultivate; I watch her remember those teenage years when I wouldn't eat except to purge.

Is she disappointed that I'm thin? Is she jealous? Is she worried about me? What do I want her to be?

"Hey 'Lize." Chase and I hug awkwardly. If there were anything interesting about Chase at all, here is where I would mention it.

There's a lounge on the mezzanine with wide chairs and low tables and bowls of wasabi peas, so we decide to sit down and get some ginger ale, let Chase and Annie catch their breath, and then they want to go to my loft apartment. I hear all about their flight and taxi ride as we establish ourselves at one of the modules and wait like rajahs for someone to come ask how they can help us.

That's when I hit them with the change of plans.

"So listen, I was hoping we could go to my place tomorrow night instead, because I was asking people if they were going to be around, and literally none of my roommates are going to be home tonight, which is so strange, it never happens, there's usually at least five or six people in the apartment at all times. I mean, I want to show you the place, but I also want you to get to meet, like, at least one of my roommates. We don't socialize a lot, but they're cool people."

"Oh." Annie frowns, skeptical. I manage not to trip on the fact that she doesn't trust me right off the bat, because I've got this great follow-up pitch.

"So I thought tonight instead we could go to the Collective, that place I was working for a while, the feminist place, remember? A few of my friends work there – I think there's a poetry reading tonight, but we could drop in and say hi. And then tomorrow, when people will be around, we'll see my place and then have dinner."

Annie raises her eyebrows and nods as she considers this. This is a fair trade. This is better than fair; this is a bonus. I hadn't mentioned taking her to the Collective as a thing that might happen; now she'll be able to add this to the list of exotic places she's been, a list that includes every single country in Epcot at Walt Disney World.

So she's happy and raring to go as we freshen up and get ready to take the New York City subway train to the Collective in Fort Greene, Brooklyn. I'm asking about things back home, and I'm getting the updates on all the serial dramas I've been watching second-hand for years. I make listening faces and listening noises, but I'm not listening.

I'm high, hyper-alert from the adrenaline. I am a genius. This is going to work. I am going to shape reality according to my wishes, like I've done so many times before. I just have to act like things are the way I want them to be, and that's how they will turn out. It's the law of positive attraction.

The Collective is only a half block from the subway stop, and it glows in the dusk of evening as we approach it. I'm narrating the story of how I first found the place, when I realize, tonight isn't poetry night. Tonight is...

Knitting night. How could I forget? Lila went on a knitting kick two or three months ago, and started a "punk rock" knitting group, whatever that means. To me, it means that the noisy, distracted crowd I was counting on is now a small circle of gossiping knitters, headed by Lila herself, who simply *love* chatting with drop-ins. I'm about to start literally dragging my feet behind Annie and Chase, and then I get a text.

"Hang on a sec," I say, stopping to check it.

It's Maria. She says:

Hi, Maureen.

And Eliza dies inside me.

I pull out my razor and put it to my wrist. All I have to do is break the skin; the Warfarin will do the rest.

Chase, in his benevolent Southern sexism, has opened the door for Annie, and my mom is stepping into the bright room full of friendly young women knitting. I can see part of the circle through the front window: Lila, Maria, Christine, Desia, and three or four random knitters – including, most randomly of all, my roommate Odessa, wielding an extra-large pair of needles through a skein of orange yarn. Their faces all turn to the door.

"Hi!" says Annie, stepping inside. "I'm Eliza's mom, Annie!" She looks over her left shoulder, where she thinks I will be.

Her face through the window is the last thing I see before I turn and run.

PART IV

ELIZABETH

January 2015

12

Dawn

I am waiting to find out who I am.

Two days ago, the kind people here tell me, I was found collapsed on a sidewalk in the Mission District of San Francisco. I had not eaten in at least forty-eight hours, I was severely dehydrated, and it looked like I had been walking for many miles on no sleep. I was carrying nothing – no money, no ID, no phone – and when the officers asked my name, I was unable to respond. They thought I might have been drugged with Rohypnol, so I was taken to the emergency room, where it was determined that I was unharmed. I was given fluids and stabilized, then sent two buildings over to the psych ward, where I was admitted as a Jane Doe.

I remember none of this. I remember none of anything.

A fugue state, they call it. An episode of dissociation so severe that it causes amnesia, sometimes mild and temporary, sometimes so severe that the sufferer's life before the fugue is essentially lost. *Okay*, I keep saying, even though I don't fully understand, and I'm becoming frustrated. I can't remember anything that happened before I woke up yesterday in an unfamiliar room, with unfamiliar voices around me, and I was wearing a hospital gown, and it wasn't a dream, and I had no idea what was happening. None.

I started screaming in terror, and uniformed strangers rushed in to restrain and sedate me. They talked to each other and not me; they were speaking in some code. This part I remember. I was convinced that I was about to be killed for some crime I had no memory of committing, but was nonetheless sure I was guilty of, and I nearly fought my way out from under a scrum of nurses and orderlies before I was given a shot of something that made me feel like, *You know what, guys? Everything's cool. Let's not fight, let's not ever fight again, okay? I'll catch up with you after my nap.*

This time, when I awakened, I had the split second feeling that I knew where I was — that I was in "my" bed, in "my" room, though I couldn't have told you where in the world such things existed — and then the knowledge dissolved. Replacing it was the knowledge that I was strapped to the bed and unable to move. Before I could start screaming again, a woman came in and told me, "Sweetheart, we'll get you right out of those cuffs, we were afraid you were going to hurt yourself, but you're okay now." She started unbuckling the restraints around my ankles, crooning, "Okay. You're okay."

Another woman came in behind her and stood near the head of my bed. "Hi, I'm Dr. Jindal, you're at St. Francis Hospital in San Francisco, and you're fine, okay? You've been here since yesterday. You're not hurt in any way, we just needed to get some more fluids in you to help you get your bearings, and you got very agitated. Can you tell me your name?"

"Uh..." I knew the first syllable was "uh," that part came out automatically. The rest of it didn't follow. "It's, uh..."

"Okay, it's okay. We'll get it later." Dr. Jindal was looking into my eyes with a light. "Do you have a headache? Any pain or numbness, anything that doesn't feel right?"

"No," I said. My wrists were freed. I said thank you to the woman who had undone them.

She said, "You're welcome, Sweetheart."

I thought, *My name should be Sweetheart.* It sounded so good when she said it.

I was very confused and starting to be scared again. Dr. Jindal was asking me to follow the light with my eyes, then to touch my nose and then her finger and then my nose and then her finger, then to tell me how many fingers she was holding up, and when the word "four" came to me just when I needed it, before I could even ask my brain for it, it was like magic – *I know this one! Four!*

"What happened to me?"

She continued her exam, knocking my elbow with a rubber hammer, lifting my arm and letting it drop. "We think you had some kind of trauma and you're in a little bit of shock, and that's made it hard for you to remember some things."

Her tone was nonchalant. This was no problem, we'd clear it up right away. "How did I get here?"

"The police found you on the sidewalk on Mission around 16th Street. You fainted from not eating or drinking anything. Do you remember any of this? Do you remember how you got to where they found you?"

I didn't. I couldn't. And it was urgent that I figure it out. Again, I had the sense of having committed a crime I didn't remember. Somebody was coming to ask me about it, and I had to know what to say.

"Is anybody coming for me?"

"How do you mean?"

"My...mother?" I had one, right? I couldn't remember her, but that was okay. Mothers were always good. If someone was your mother, they'd come right to your bedside and fix things as soon as they arrived. This came to me the way the number four did, *a priori.*

"Can you tell us your mom's name?"

"Aah..." It started with "aah."

"Is it Lilith?"

"Lilith." *That name is important. Is she my mother? Lilith. Lilith.* "I know that name, but I don't know who she is."

"Her name is tattooed on your arm."

I raised my left arm and saw the tattoo on the shoulder, covering a thicket of old scars. The same arm had an inch long vertical scar that started about two inches under the wrist. What else did I have on me that I didn't know about?

"Okay, it's okay. We'll find everybody we can find, but right now do you feel well enough to stand up, show me how you're walking?"

Dr. Jindal stayed with me for the next half hour, asking me questions, assuring me that it was okay if I didn't know the answers. I liked her calm way of doing things. She didn't seem angry. She took the things I said seriously. She was obviously very smart, and she was going to help me, and that's what I clung to in the short term. She was my first friend. If my mother didn't show up, perhaps Dr. Jindal could take over for her.

"Okay, Kiddo," she said, finally. "Here's the deal. You're physically fine, you don't have any signs of any recent physical trauma, except from where you fell down, so nothing bad happened to you while you were unaware of it. Okay?"

Okay.

"So we're going to take you for an EEG soon to check your brain, but it looks like things are working well up there. My guess is you've been overwhelmed, fatigued, there's been some stress in your life, and you're having some temporary amnesia, but I think you're going to get over it very soon. I think things are going to start coming back to you, and then you'll recover more and more of your memory. In the meantime, rest, let your body heal. You want me to send up some Jell-O from the cafeteria?"

"Yes, please."

How did I know what Jell-O was and not know who I was? How did I know to say please? How did I know that this kind of care and attention was what I'd been looking for my whole life, when I couldn't remember a minute of it?

Because I am white, I am considered worthy of a mention on the local news. They show a drawing of me; it looks like a court reporter's sketch. I have no idea how that happened. I am called the "Mystery Girl of the Mission." Anyone with any information is encouraged to call the police.

A billion people call the police. It turns out that a billion people are just waiting for the invitation to call the police about anything at all. It's going to take a while to sort through the crackpots; the most credible candidates will be screened further before I'm asked to speak to them. I'm eager to find out who I am, but I am not eager to endure this Rorschach test of being bombarded with people to see what atavistic reaction they inspire in me.

Dr. Jindal and Dr. Brouillard are hoping that my memory will return organically. They emphasize the importance of patience and positive thinking – "You *will* recover from this." I *will* recover from this. It's been suggested that if I can just rest, not force myself to remember anything, but maybe look at the television, or these magazines, and maybe something will remind me of something...

I watch TV with the other patients in the lounge. They seem very much like children to me – not unintelligent, just young. I suppose I'm the same. We need structure, routine, activities, boundaries, the security of knowing that someone else is in charge. We require a lot of patience and soothing tones, then we get angry for being patronized.

"Are you a junkie?" asks Dean, who is here to adjust the meds for his manic depression. "You look like a junkie but you don't, and you don't have the needle-needle-needle marks. If you're a junkie, you're in the *wroooong plaaaace*." He draws this out, shaking his head no.

"I don't think I'm a junkie," I say, and my brain goes through its addled machinations. Junket: a trip you take for work; junk: a type of boat; junkle: that's not a thing. Needle marks...that's from drugs...junkie...is a heroin addict! "No," I say, triumphant and relieved. "I'm not a junkie."

"You're a junkie," he says, dismissive. "You're in the *wroooong plaaaace*."

Claudia stands in front of Dean, blocking his view of the TV. "Leave her alone, she doesn't know anything." She turns to me. "What I wouldn't give. You think amnesia is contagious? I need some of that. Too much memory is what I got. I'll give you half of mine, you give me some of what you got."

"Amnesia," I say. It's a word I'm hearing a lot.

"Like Fred Flintstone," Claudia says. "Remember he got hit on the head with a rock, and he thought he was some rich guy?"

"Yes," I say, because that sounds familiar, and I want to be agreeable.

"You remember Fred Flintstone but you don't remember your own name! Hey, maybe your name is Mickey Mouse!" Claudia laughs for a second before it turns into a honking cough. She gathers her sputum in her chest.

"No spitting," warns Yveline. She is the nurse who unlocked me from my bed, so I consider her my other best friend, after Dr. Jindal, and before Nellie who brings the trays of food. "Go spit in the toilet if you must."

Claudia spits at the corner, then starts heading back to her room. "What you gotta do is, hit your head with the rock again, and you'll go back to being Fred Flintstone."

I wander back to my room. It is the only thing that feels at all familiar. I look at myself in the reflection of the window, wearing the dirty black t-shirt and jeans that are "mine." It's cheap clothing from national chains, no clues that would help determine its provenance, no particular style beyond "anonymous tomboy." No jewelry, though my ears have several piercings apiece. My hair is clipped short and my tattoo says Lilith. I'm going to go out on a limb and guess that I'm gay.

I'm becoming comfortable here, which I am told is unusual. Most people don't like being in the hospital. Maybe it's my lack of other alternatives, but I don't mind being here. It's nice, having people keep track of me so I don't wander off like a toddler in a supermarket. It feels natural to me to be here, maybe because this is all I remember.

Maybe I lived in a hospital in my former life.

Dr. Jindal tells me not to think of it as my "former" life – it's still my life, it's waiting for me, and I will find it or it will find me soon enough. I don't know. This new life is growing on me. I don't seem to miss anybody from my life before this week; I'm not yearning to be reunited with anyone, or to restart a vocation or hobby. I still have this nagging fear that I did something bad that I'm going to be held accountable for.

You could look at this whole amnesia thing as a gift.

"A fresh start," says a voice in my mind that's not mine.

―――――

What do you think about, when you have no memories to reflect upon? No grudges to nurse, no joys to relive, no moments

of recalled embarrassment that make you wince decades later?
What do you think about when you're in the moment?

I marvel at the world. I marvel at the way windows work,
everything about them: glass that comes from sand, air that
moves as wind, we call this a sash and that a squirrel. I can see
clearly now, the pane is clean. Everything is interesting: the little
pencil they give me to check off my choices on the menu – why
that small and no smaller? Who decides these things? The silver
hat that comes on top of the plate to keep it warm.

"Look," I say to the woman in the other bed. I think her name
is Riva. "It's a hat for food."

I say things simultaneous to thinking them, and I notice it
simultaneously, and I notice that I notice it. There is a special
name for this infinite mirror effect, but I can't remember it now.
And how do mirrors work, anyway? I was trying to figure it out
in the bathroom; I was going to take the mirror off the wall,
but it turns out you can't do that in the psych ward. In fact,
our mirrors are some kind of non-breakable non-mirrors that
barely cast a reflection – it's like trying to see yourself in the side
of a toaster, which is even more disconcerting when you keep
needing to be reminded what you look like.

Riva grunts. She does not seem to be aware that she is a
galaxy of intricate physics. There are so many separate entities
and forces that have to collide in exactly the right way to keep
the Riva-machine working: all these interdependent organs that
sift various substances from various others, all those electrons
spinning and bonding and coming unbound, some ineffable
"spirit" or "life" that she is imbued with, the near-zero
coincidence that any of this exists at all. Spectacular. I am a
miracle myself – have you ever really looked at your hand?

Whatever happens from here, I hope I get to keep this awe
and reverence. I hope I never get jaded. I never want to stop
marveling at my own hand ("Junkie," says Dean), the way it can
feel things like temperature and weight and texture all at once,
even when I'm not paying attention. I spend twenty minutes
touching one hand lightly with the other, feeling both things at
the same time: my fingers touching, my fingers being touched. I
spend another twenty standing in front of the sink moving my

fingers under the stream of water, watching it rope around my hand.

And people – you hopeful, pitiable, existentially outmatched creatures. I could watch you for hours. A brisk woman named Irma comes in to change my bed sheets, and every one of her movements is efficient. Everything she does works. There is no dropping things, no pillows that refuse to lay flush in their cases; when she snaps a sheet, it snaps to. I am mesmerized. She sees me watching, and does not slow down or do anything differently, but there is extra flourish to her exactitude. This feels like an act of love between us, her skill, my appreciation, and I am unreasonably happy to be sitting in a visitor's chair witnessing the changing of my sheets.

But when Irma walks out of the room (and ceases to exist, inasmuch as I know), wherever she goes, she is Irma. She never gets to be anybody else. She will always be brisk; she will always be the kind of smart and watchful person who seems to be biding her time while waiting for the bullshit to die down. Whatever fears she had when she came into the room are with her on her way out, whatever ailments, grievances and loves. The same tics, the same sayings, never anything but that. She never gets to see through new eyes.

She never gets to shed her history. But she doesn't need to. She is okay with being Irma, and when she's not, she's made peace with it.

Everybody brings their whirligig personalities into the room with them, like a propeller on top of a beanie. They're celebrity guest stars in the show I watch from my bed, appearing as themselves. I want to applaud for them when they come in and out of the room. *Yay, it's Yveline, and she's going to say Yveline things.* I love the face she makes when she says hello to someone else, and the face she makes right afterwards.

It's wonderful to be nobody, to have no role to play or expectations to fulfill. I don't need to have a personality, I can just watch and be. And I am overcome with such tenderness for everyone: the guy who changes out the garbage bags, the woman who visits Riva every other day. I want to stop everyone and say, *Hey, I see you, and you're doing a great job being a person.*

Thank you for persevering in the face of existential terror and mortal loss. I will be very sad when this ends, as it must, because soon my identity will be established and I'll have to go back to being that one person all the time, forever. I have a feeling that's going to be a problem.

———

Maureen the social worker says they think they have found my mother.

I hope they have, because I know I can't stay here indefinitely, and the options available to me are not ideal – group homes, assisted living. I don't need any assistance with living, thanks, just some help getting on my feet. I'm told I'll need to get a new identity and a new birth certificate so I can apply for public assistance, and I feel so overwhelmed by the idea of all of it; I just want to say, *I'm sorry, I have amnesia. Can I go lie down now?*

Maureen brings the mother into the private conference room where I am waiting with Dr. Jindal, Dr. Brouillard, and two other doctors who have been consulting on the case. The mother is a pretty, fiftyish white woman in a blue shirt-dress and espadrilles. Her hair is dark blonde with some grey streaks, pulled back into a bun. She is shaking. She has tears in her hazel eyes.

"Hello, Mom," I say politely. I think this is right. They tell me this is right. She is my mother, Annabel Madigan. My name is Elizabeth Madigan.

"Elizabeth." The woman holds out her arms to embrace me. She is almost exactly my height. Do we look alike? I can't tell, because she is hugging me and crying on me. I pat her back supportively. Poor woman. I can't imagine what she's been through. "Oh, Elizabeth."

She draws back and waits for me to recognize her. We're all waiting: me, the mother, Dr. Jindal, Maureen, etc.

Everything is familiar, I just can't place it.

"You don't remember me yet," says the woman, trying to put a smile on top of her grief. She doesn't want me to feel bad for

198 | I, Liar

dashing her hopes. She's knows it's not my fault. I want to tell her that I appreciate her sensitivity, and I can see she must be a very generous and sympathetic person, to consider the feelings of a stranger at a time like this.

We seat ourselves next to each other at the table. "I'm sorry," I say.

"That's okay, Honey. I'm just so glad you're all right. I thought...I might not see you again..." She breaks down into a sob that becomes a laugh. "I'm so grateful you're okay."

I'll admit it, I'm flattered. She's concerned about me, she's happy I'm alive – what more does anyone want from a mother? "Thank you," I say.

She puts her right hand on my left forearm. I can feel not just warmth, but a buzz. I hear her breath, I hear her stomach, I hear her blood. Her touch has a meaning. This hasn't happened with anybody else who's touched me since I've been here.

The mother brought pictures to show me: a baby being held by a middle-aged woman standing next to a man. "There you are with your grandparents," she tells me. "Doreen and Joe. We lived with them in Florida until you were four years old. You and your grandmother just adored each other. My father was more difficult. I think he scared you. He was angry at me, and you picked up on it. You were very sensitive to things like that."

"Yes," I say. This sounds plausible. This man looks like he could have been frightening to a child. His stare is uncanny; it's like he can see me from inside the photo. Yes, he's angry, he feels cheated of something he knows isn't his. He would murder someone, if he could figure out who.

She's brought a handkerchief with some of the cologne he used to wear; she withdraws it from its plastic bag and offers it to me and I take it, and again I think, *Yes.* If that man were transposed into a smell, this would be him.

I return the handkerchief to her. "Why was he angry at you?"

"Well...I became pregnant out of wedlock. And I was unable to identify the father."

"What do you mean?"

This is a hard story for her to tell in the presence of the shrinks. What is she, fifty? And she's still ashamed of things that happened decades ago. I want to place my hand on her arm the way she did to mine, and – *bzzzzzt!* – make it better.

"Well, the man who was your father was married when we met. I knew it at the time, he didn't lie to me. He didn't pretend he was leaving his wife. He was very up front about his feelings. When I got pregnant, he said he wanted nothing to do with a child, and he didn't want me to keep it, but if I did, I should 'keep it away from him.'"

My God! "What an *asshole*," I say sincerely.

She laughs, dabs her eyes with a tissue, turns to her purse to put away the handkerchief that smells of her late father's cologne and hides her face for a moment, but I see it. She is *in extremis*. Her face is contorted with a lifetime's worth of sadness, regret, self-loathing, shame. She loved this man, she even made herself a mistress to be with him, and she didn't get loved in return. She thinks this is her fault, a punishment for wanting the wrong thing.

The mother raises her head, smiles, and continues. "So I told my father I didn't know who the father was, and I stuck to that story, and I never contacted him again. And when you started asking about who your father was, I told you the same thing: I didn't know.

"That was wrong. I think you were hurt by that. You never stopped wanting a father. But I didn't know what to do. He didn't want anything to do with you, and I was so hurt and outraged on your behalf, I thought, 'He'll never get to see her. He'll never get to make her feel the way he made me feel.'"

I like the fuck-you spirit in her voice when she says this. I like the way she wanted to protect her daughter – me – from hurt and rejection. My father was not a nice guy, not a good person; he was a selfish, lying manipulator. You have to steer clear of people like that.

I wonder if she knows where he is these days, and when I will get around to being interested enough to pursue the subject. Right now, I am wholly invested in this mother-person, whose own smell is starting to feel familiar – not because I've ever smelled it before today, but because over the last ten minutes, this woman has come to mean a great deal to me.

"So then what happened?"

"Your grandfather died of a stroke when you were six, and two years later, your grandmother was diagnosed with breast cancer and had her surgeries. You and I were living in New Jersey at the time, but we went back to Florida to stay with her for a few months during her surgery. By then, she was in Clearwater."

She produces another photo: a girl in a pool at an apartment complex, hair smeared across her face, random elderly ankles in the background. It takes me a moment to recognize myself, but then it registers, *That's me.* I smell chlorine, feel my fingertips pucker.

"You spent a lot of time with her in the hospital. You were like a little nurse; you got water for Grandma, you helped her fill out her menu, you shushed people when she was sleeping. You were so bright, you picked up all the medical terms right away. Everybody said you could be a doctor when you grew up." She smiles. I can't tell if it's rue or pride.

"I shouldn't have let you spend so much time there. You were eight, you shouldn't have been hanging around a cancer ward. But it was so good for your grandmother to have you there. And I thought, 'Who knows how much longer she's going to be around? Let them spend time together while they can.' I didn't realize…" She pauses, looking for the right way to put it. "I think it…affected you."

The pause – it's not good. She's holding something back. Everything she's said so far has been a relief to both of us. What doesn't she want to say?

"What do you mean?"

Again, she hesitates. "Well, I think…sometimes you felt…"

I'm stricken with sympathetic agitation: throat tight, sternum aching. She's afraid of me. The mother is afraid of me. And I thought we were getting along so well – I didn't know her, but I liked her. I trusted her. She was overjoyed to find her missing daughter alive, and I was excited to be the daughter that brought her joy.

"What did I do?" I ask.

She shakes her head, won't meet my eye. "It wasn't you, Honey. You were unhappy, you were reacting to things…I should have understood you better…"

"What do you mean…"

The mother looks at the scar on the inside of my left forearm. Oh, right. I've discussed this scar with Dr. Jindal. It's only a few months old, and too small to have done real damage. Dr. Jindal says it's probably the same thing that caused me to slit my wrist that's causing this fugue. Not an incentive for me to recover my memory.

"I did everything I could think of," pleads the mother. She looks at me, at the doctors, back to me. "We sent you to psychiatrists, you went to a treatment clinic...I didn't know what to do. You were cutting yourself, you made yourself sick...you weren't even thirteen when it started."

I reach over and fondle the old scars under my tattoo, seeking comfort. I don't like this line of conversation. It's upsetting her and that's upsetting me. I was feeling close to the mother, and now she's getting farther away. "I'm sorry," I say.

"No, Lizzybit." Now she's crying, shielding her eyes with one hand. "I'm sorry. It wasn't your fault. Whatever I did, it wasn't enough."

The name Lizzybit rings a bell. A door opens inside me, through which enters unease. "It's okay," I say. "It doesn't matter now."

I wish the mother would look at me, reach out for me. Be happy, the way she was when she first saw me.

"It's okay," I say again. "It doesn't matter any more. It's in the past."

I pull my chair right up to hers, aching to be embraced. She looks up from her sobbing and sees me there.

Please, I think. Love me.

I offer her my scarred arms, and she takes me in. Her heart beats against my chest, her cheek is wet against mine. She pets my hair and says *shhhh* and we cry on each other like one person in two parts. I am finally where I am meant to be.

And when she pulls away from me, I feel forsaken, overtaken by a vertiginous falling forward. A dawning horror rushes over me like water over a boat, and I'm drowning in a flood of flashes:

A young girl digs alone at the base of a tree by a playground, walks along a parkway in the parching sun. A tray of melted cupcakes in the garbage.

A girl sits alone in a strange room, the shrill song of a modem connecting, her shoulder stinging. You have no new mail.

A girl lies alone in a dorm room listening to the music of people talking next door. The sound of her name spoken, then laughs.

A girl thrashes in a hospital bed, choking on the charcoal foaming from her throat. The overlooked note waiting unread at home.

A girl runs up and down a staircase until she vomits, then runs up and down some more. A phone and a text and who is this, who are you, is anybody there?

The girl chases other girls and catches them by the hair and bites their skull and it's not a dream this time.

Please don't let this happen. Please don't let this be true. I don't want this to be true. I can't go back to being me, not after the rapture of losing myself like I did. I can't.

There's nothing to do but what I've always done.

I hold my breath, stand up quickly, and pass out.

I come to in a hospital bed with the taste of Novocain and three stitches inside my mouth. I must have punctured my cheek when my head hit the table. Hovering above me are a doctor and a nurse.

"Where...where am I?"

The doctor, a woman, says, "Elizabeth, you're in St. Francis Hospital, you were having some temporary amnesia and you fainted – do you remember any of this?"

"Hospital?" I ask, astonished. "Amnesia?"

"Elizabeth?" I hear another woman's voice in the background. "Are you all right?"

I look right at the strange woman. "Who are you?" I ask. "Where am I?"

It's called anterograde amnesia. When I first came to St. Francis, I was suffering from retrograde amnesia, where you can't remember anything from the past, but you can create new memories in the present. When I fainted, it developed into anterograde amnesia, where you can't even form new memories. I can barely recall basic things from one minute to the next.

In order to cope with this disorder, I keep a small notebook with me at all times, with the most delightful teeny tiny pencil to write things down. It keeps me from asking simple questions again and again. The doctors say I'm going to require a long period of adjustment, which I will spend at a nursing home, where this kind of memory loss is *de rigeur*.

I will have therapists working with me for hours every day, and counselors to talk to about whatever I want. I'm getting a private nurse, so I don't have to rely on an overworked staff. My mother will be there, supporting my recovery. I will be taken care of 24 hours a day until I'm able to function on my own.

Perhaps someday I will be able to overcome the trauma that caused my amnesia in the first place, and my memories will return, along with my ability to make new memories, and I will be able to live a normal, productive life like everyone else.

I can only hope.

———————

I never told you what happened in Vancouver, did I.
But that was the old me.

Thanks

Mink Choi, Kaitlyn Wylde, and Thought Catalog Books
Eric Nelson
Bruce Tracy
Koren Zailckas
Caitlin Schoenfeld
Anne Elliott
Melissa Febos
Friends: David Brouillard, Jennifer Dziura, Adam Schoenfeld, Dana Piccoli, Lana Lauriano, Jennifer Sanders Weiner, Erik Seims, Melissa Roth, Anne Sussman, Emilie Blythe McDonald, Satia Cecil, Chris Donovan
Dr. Robin Young
Larry Erlbaum
Bill Scurry

About the Author

Janice Erlbaum is the author of two memoirs, *Girlbomb: A Halfway Homeless Memoir* (Villard/Random House, 2006), and *Have You Found Her* (Villard/Random House, 2008). She lives with her husband in her native New York City, where she teaches writing. She can be found at www.girlbomb.com.

Made in the USA
Middletown, DE
05 July 2015